3

E-BOY

ANH DO

3

ENTER THE JUNGLE

E-BOY

Illustrations by Chris Wahl

ALLEN&UNWIN

SYDNEY•MELBOURNE•AUCKLAND•LONDON

First published by Allen & Unwin in 2021

Text copyright © Anh Do, 2021
Illustrations by Chris Wahl, 2021

All rights reserved. No part of this book may be reproduced or
transmitted in any form or by any means, electronic or mechanical,
including photocopying, recording or by any information storage
and retrieval system, without prior permission in writing from
the publisher. The Australian *Copyright Act 1968* (the Act) allows a
maximum of one chapter or ten per cent of this book, whichever is
the greater, to be photocopied by any educational institution for
its educational purposes provided that the educational institution
(or body that administers it) has given a remuneration notice to the
Copyright Agency (Australia) under the Act.

Allen & Unwin
83 Alexander Street
Crows Nest NSW 2065
Australia
Phone: (61 2) 8425 0100
Email: info@allenandunwin.com
Web: www.allenandunwin.com

A catalogue record for this
book is available from the
National Library of Australia

ISBN 978 1 76087 902 0

For teaching resources, explore www.allenandunwin.com/resources/
for-teachers

Cover design by Jo Hunt and Chris Wahl
Text design by Jo Hunt
Set in 13/22 pt Legacy Serif by Jo Hunt

Printed and bound in Australia by McPherson's Printing Group

10 9 8 7 6 5 4 3 2 1

The paper in this book is FSC® certified.
FSC® promotes environmentally responsible,
socially beneficial and economically viable
management of the world's forests.

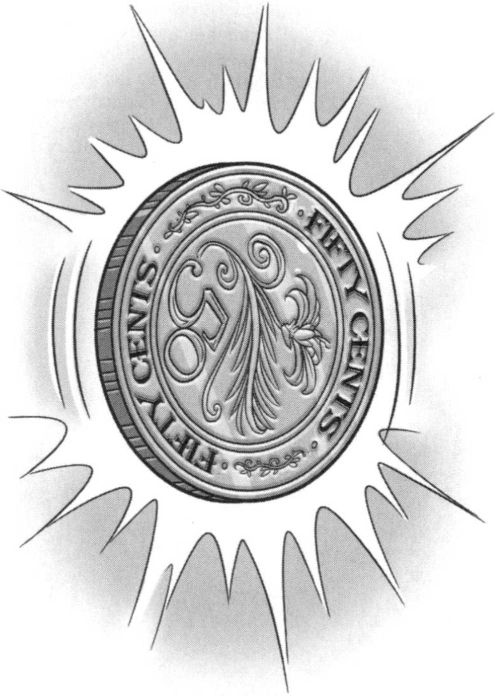
FIFTY CENTS
FIFTY CENTS
50

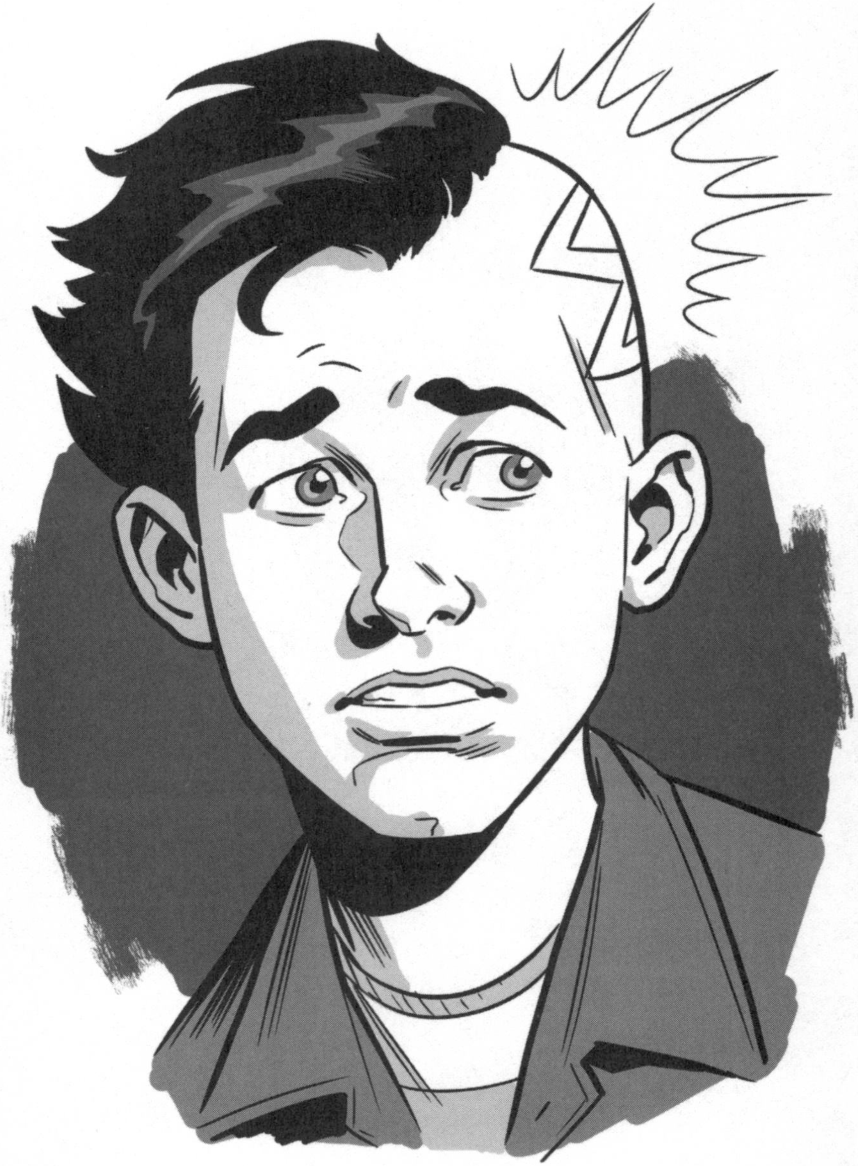

CHAPTER 1

Ethan was worried.

He'd been worried ever since his parents had sent a short, panicked email.

Mum and Dad

...dangerous for us to stay here.
We need help son.
                    -Mum and Dad

He immediately drove to the airport, abandoned the sports car in the carpark, and ran inside. As soon as he was in range of airport wi-fi, Ethan booked himself a seat on the next flight to Esconda.

Since Ethan didn't have his helmet on, the National Service couldn't know what he looked like, so he was able to sneak through Customs without raising any alarms. Even so, he kept his head down.

He was thinking about Penny.

The fact that Penny had chosen the robot Gemini over him still stung.

Ethan couldn't sit still, pacing around the terminal until it came time to board the flight.

The plane eventually landed in the tiny country of Esconda. Ethan was nervous as he made his way through the airport, but there were enough signs in English for him to find the taxi rank. Twenty minutes later, his cab arrived at the Sandpiper Resort.

Ethan messaged his parents during the drive, and as the cab pulled into the resort driveway Tracy and Paul Forrester ran out to meet him.

They hugged him tight, all of them crying in relief at seeing each other again. No one wanted to let go, until the taxi gave an impatient honk.

Ethan looked sheepish. 'Uh . . . sorry, but I don't have any cash for the cab.'

Ethan's parents looked at each other gravely, and Paul dashed back into the resort. Tracy saw the puzzled look on Ethan's face.

'It's dangerous to carry cash around at the moment, Ethan,' Tracy explained. 'That's the reason why we contacted you.'

'Are you both okay?' Ethan said, confused.

'Yes, love, but we can't stay here. Crime is going up in a hurry, and it's mainly because of one man.'

Paul came back and handed the taxi driver a couple of notes. 'Sorry about the wait. Keep the change.'

The driver took the cash and sped away.

'Because of who?' asked Ethan.

'A criminal called Money Man,' said Paul.

CHAPTER 2

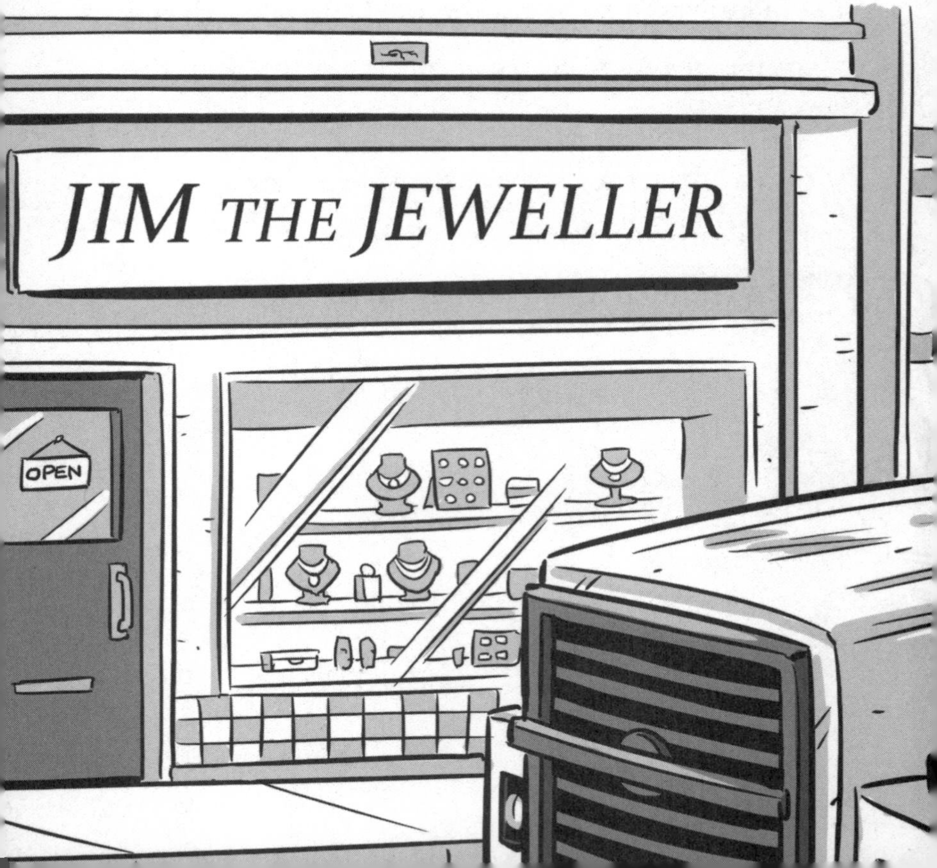
JIM THE JEWELLER
OPEN

The story of Esconda's most famous criminal started long before Paul and Tracy Forrester arrived.

Six years earlier, Chaz Checkman was a tow-truck driver. For a while his business was doing okay, but it wasn't enough for Chaz. He'd grown up poor and now that he could buy flashy things, he did.

He bought jewellery and expensive clothes, fancy TVs, a sound system and a jetski. He bought and bought and spent much more money than he made.

He borrowed money to buy more luxuries, and in order to pay people back he couldn't afford to keep his truck serviced. It started to break down during pickups, which cost him money, which meant he had to borrow more.

One night, as he had just come off a shift, he saw an ATM in a wall that looked cracked and insecure. Chaz thought about his debts, and his expensive tastes, and hooked his tow truck up to the ATM. *There's enough cash in one of these to last me for ages!* he thought.

He revved the engine hard, and the tyres spun and squealed against the road until with a CRUNCH the ATM came away.

The sound of alarms filled the night as Chaz loaded the ATM onto the back of his truck. His plan was working – until he tried to start his truck.

'C'mon, you silly thing! Don't break down on me now!'

Kunk kunk kunk kunk kunk

The truck just wouldn't fire up! All it did was make the awful noise it made when it didn't want to start.

KUNK
KUNK
KUNK KUNK

Chaz climbed out of the truck and lifted the bonnet. 'C'mon!!!' he screamed as he jiggled some wires around the engine.

Suddenly . . . *VROOM!* The truck roared to life.

'Yes!' exclaimed Chaz.

He jumped back into his truck and sped away. But as he rounded the first corner, the steering failed and he ran straight into a power pole. In no time at all he was surrounded by police.

Chaz went to jail.

On his first day in the small, dingy, smelly prison cell, Chaz's eye was caught by a glint of reflected light in a dark corner, and he found a fifty-cent piece. It seemed a strange find, as no prisoners were allowed to have cash on them. He picked it up.

Well, he thought, *if I'm going to get back to buying luxuries when I'm out, I'm going to need to start somewhere ...*

He served his sentence quietly, and after four years he was released. As he stood at the exit, he was given his clothes and belongings back – and also some bad news.

'The prison bus is getting serviced, so it can't take you back into town today,' a guard told him.

Chaz's shoulders slumped.

'Are you sure you can't call anyone to pick you up?' asked the guard.

Chaz just shook his head. He had no family, and he'd borrowed money from all of his friends without repaying them. So when he went to jail, they wanted nothing more to do with him.

'You could stay here tonight – the bus should be fixed tomorrow.'

'Back in a cell? No chance. I need to be outside these walls. I'll walk it.'

'It's about thirty kilometres!' said the guard.

'Then I'd better get started,' said Chaz.

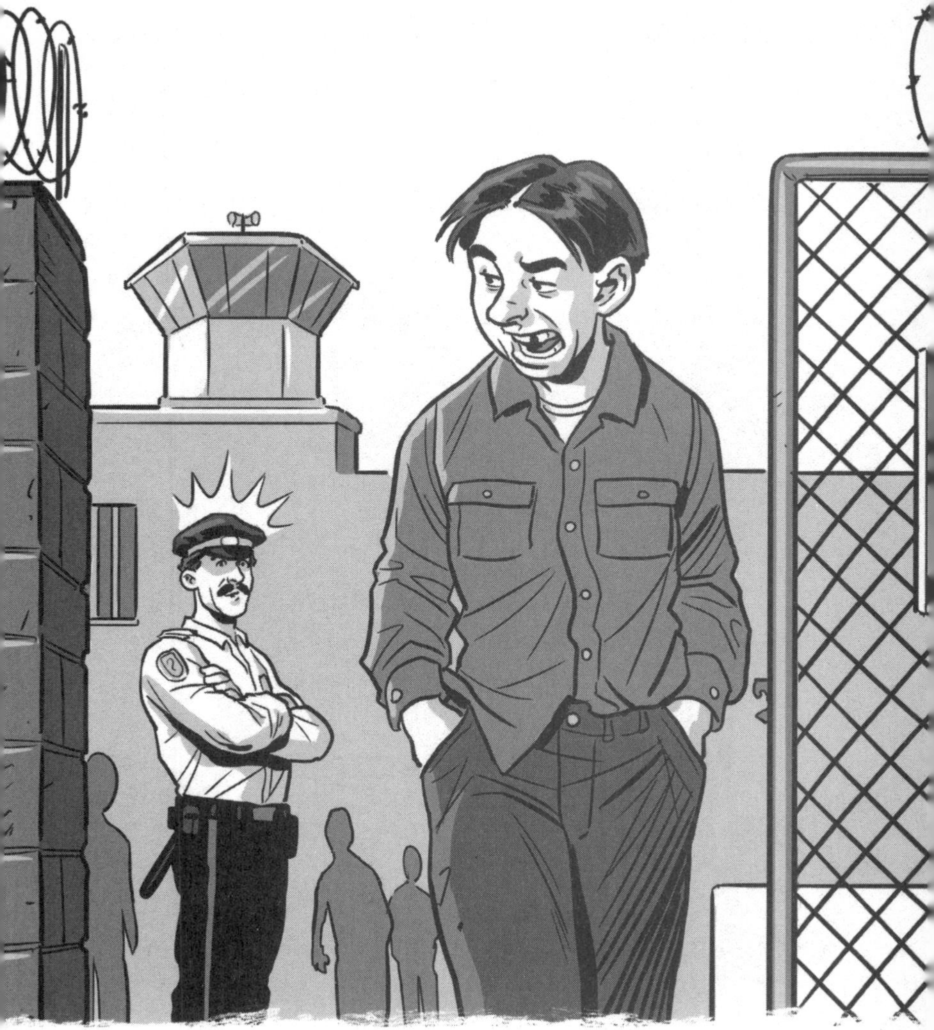

Chaz walked along the highway as the sun began to set. He tried hitchhiking for a while, but no one was going to stop and pick anyone up from the road that passed the prison. The daylight drained away but Chaz trudged on.

After a few more hours, the highway went up a hill, and from there Chaz could see the lights of the city in the distance. As he stood, seeing just how far he still had to go, the effort of the walk caught up with him and he sagged with exhaustion.

He weighed up whether to continue or find a tree to fall asleep under. Just as he pulled out his favourite coin to toss to help him make up his mind, he spotted a tiny purple light in the sky ahead.

The light came rushing towards him with a high whooshing noise. Chaz stood transfixed as it approached, until a small, glowing purple rock sped past his head and smashed into a nearby tree. The impact sprayed Chaz with bark and flecks of purple goo, which he wiped off his hands instinctively.

Chaz looked at the tree – it had been split in half. And the impact seemed to have destroyed the rock, leaving only a few globs of the goo. As he watched, stunned, those globs sank out of sight into the tree and earth.

Well, I guess I'm walking a bit further, thought Chaz. *I don't want to sleep near that!*

Chaz set off again, but less than an hour later he could continue no further. He found a patch of soft ground under a tree, and lay down to rest.

As he slept he dreamed of his fifty-cent piece growing, and multiplying, until he had a whole house and furniture made out of coins.

Chaz woke up with the sun, coin clutched in hand. He was still tired – slumping against a tree had made for a broken night's sleep. As he took his first few steps back onto the highway, he stumbled, and the coin flew out of his hand and started rolling down the hill. He reached for it, just out of instinct . . .

. . . and it flew back to him!

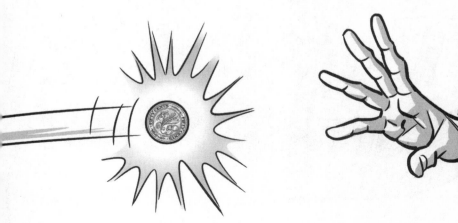

He stared at the coin, thinking he must still be dreaming. *What the?* he thought. *There's no way that this coin really changed direction and flew back into my hand.*

He shook his head and continued along the highway, but just a few steps further, he stopped.

He looked at the coin again, then threw it into the air. It flipped a few times and fell down at his feet. He picked the coin up and threw it into the air again, then concentrated.

The coin stopped in mid-air!

Chaz kept concentrating, and the fifty-cent piece turned one way, then another, up, down, looping around. And then it flew back into his hand.

Chaz let out a shocked giggle.

Maybe it's not just this coin. He pulled his wallet from his pocket, and took out the two five-dollar notes and single ten-cent piece that had sat in there for four years. With merely a thought, he plucked them from the wallet without touching them. They danced around his hand, making him almost giddy with delight.

He even folded one note into a paper plane and sent it soaring, chasing after a blackbird, while he clapped and danced like a three-year-old.

As Chaz walked on, playing with his new abilities, he arrived at the outskirts of town, barely noticing the last few kilometres. Once he saw more buildings and fewer trees, though, his feet started to hurt. He thought about hailing a taxi, but ten dollars wouldn't get him far.

I wonder...

He saw a man jogging nearby, expensive headphones covering his ears, with a tiny poodle on a leash struggling to keep up. The jogger sneered at the layers of dirt covering Chaz because of his long trek. Chaz looked at the jogger's pockets – none of them was bulging enough to be carrying a wallet.

But Chaz thought he caught a glimpse of a money clip.

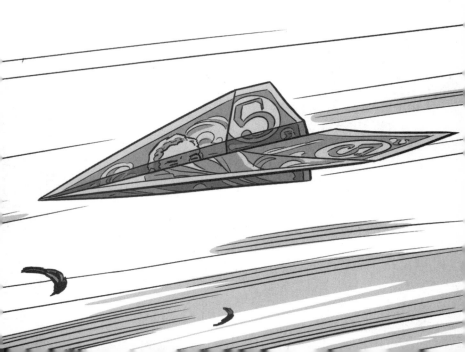

He looked around to make sure no one else was watching, and, just as the jogger stepped onto the road, Chaz made a small tugging gesture with his hand. The money clip flew out of the jogger's pocket and into Chaz's grasp.

The jogger paused in the middle of the road, unsure whether or not he'd felt something, then turned and continued his run.

Chaz let out another giggle, then counted his windfall. It was only forty-five dollars, but it was forty-five dollars he didn't have a minute ago.

'TAXI!'

Chaz stole his way back to comfort. He would follow someone in expensive clothing, and when they were busy or distracted he would lift a note or two from their wallet or pocket, sending them directly into his own.

One thing prison had taught Chaz was patience. Over the next couple of years he collected millions, a few notes at a time. He tried using his powers on other valuables, diamonds and jewellery, but they only worked on cash.

Eventually the tax department started asking awkward questions about where Chaz's money

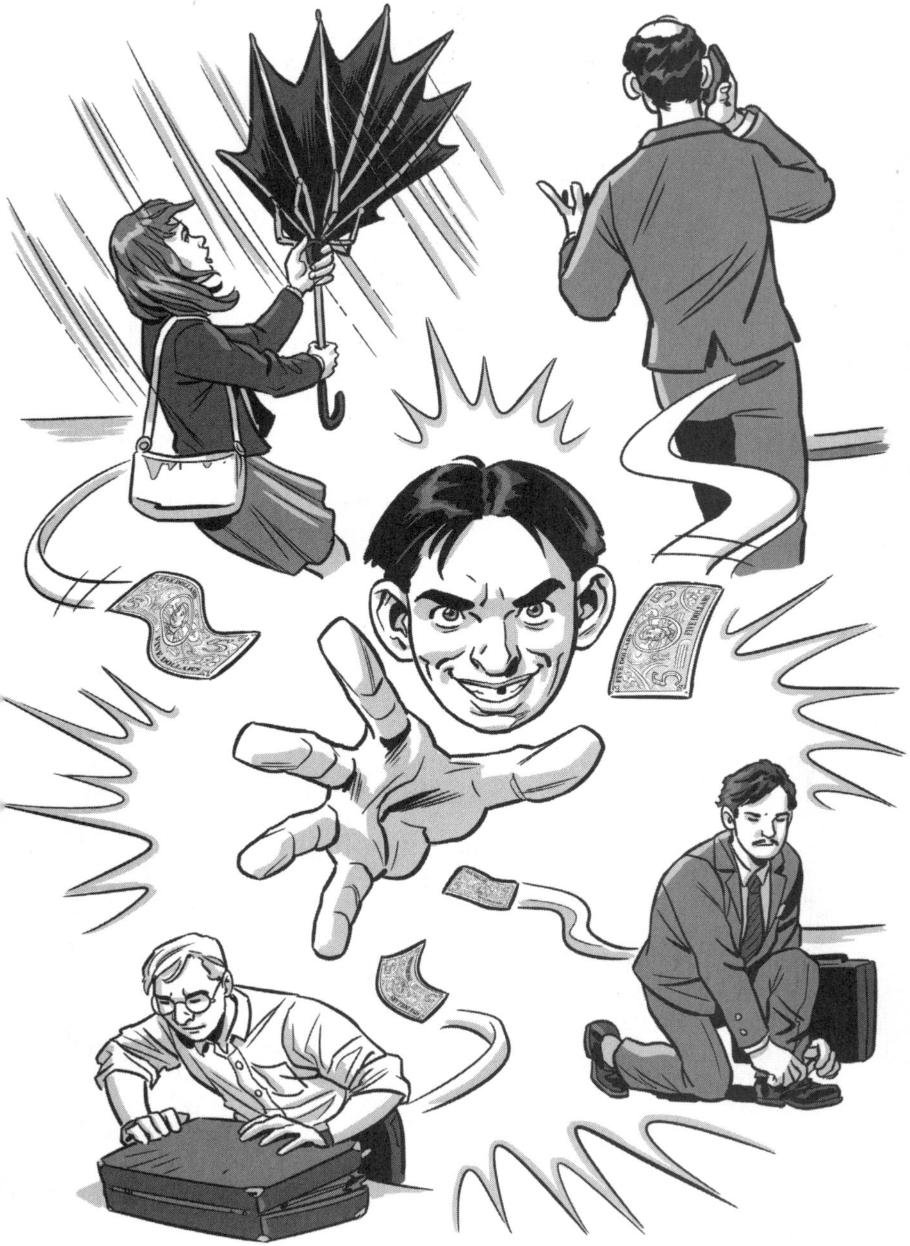

was coming from. Chaz made plans to leave Titus and head to where the tax laws were a lot more relaxed, and where there were lots of rich people to lift cash from.

Esconda.

With a new home, Chaz decided to take on a new life. Well, two, really. He used his stolen riches to build a mansion with two distinct halves. One half was the public face belonging

to Chaz Checkman, multimillionaire. It was filled with furniture and art that was obviously expensive, but not too outrageous.

The other, secret half of the mansion belonged to Chaz's new criminal identity: the super-powered Money Man. Everything was lined with gold and jewels. Thick wads of cash sat on marble tables. Even the toilets were pure gold.

Chaz looked like a respectable businessman. Just to keep up appearances he even rented an office that he went into most days, where he did almost nothing. But when he donned his mask, white fur coat, thick gold chains, gold-plated top hat and glasses with dollar signs on the lenses, Money Man struck fear into the hearts of the rich people of Esconda.

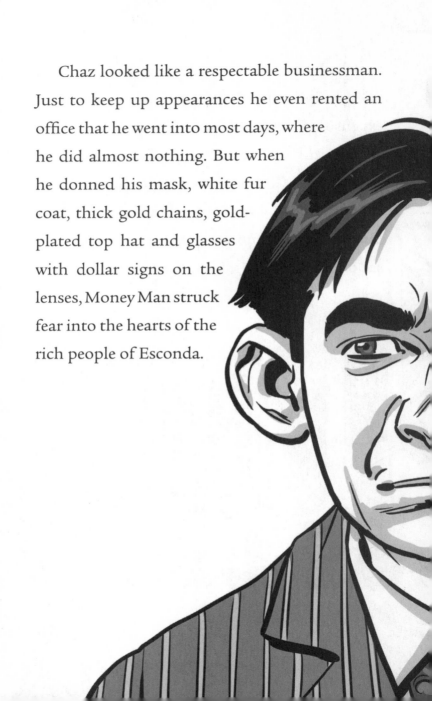

Money Man would boldly rob people, or a business, casually flick a few notes to any poor people who might be nearby, and vanish back into Chaz's respectable life. People argued about whether he was a heartless criminal or a dashing rogue.

For a while, anyway.

CHAPTER 3

Ethan sat on the couch in his parents' room at the resort, listening to them describe Money Man's spate of robberies.

'The thing is,' said Paul, 'rich people here just gave up carrying cash and started paying for everything with credit cards. Money Man doesn't stop, though – he just targets poorer people now. Everyone's jumpy. It's been nice here, but maybe we could . . . come home?'

Ethan looked at his dad with sad eyes. 'I'm sorry . . . I'm really sorry, but it's still too dangerous.'

'Is that why Doctor Penny isn't with you?' Paul asked. 'Is she—'

'Can we not talk about her right now?' snapped Ethan.

There was an awkward pause in the conversation. Ethan's mum patted him on the knee and said, 'Look, we can talk about this later. We haven't seen each other for the longest time – let's go out for a nice dinner and figure some things out in the morning.'

Ethan's dad brightened. 'There's a great restaurant around the corner. Let's go.'

Fifteen minutes later, the Forrester family were sitting around a table in El Delicioso, chatting and laughing over a platter of chicken enchiladas.

Paul said, 'Hey Ethan, what about that time you a gobbled a huge hunk of wasabi thinking it was avocado dip?'

Tracy laughed and Ethan laughed even louder.

'You looked like you were going to explode!' Paul said. They were the loudest table in the restaurant, but no one seemed to mind. Their good mood was infectious.

Then the door opened.

Standing in the doorway was a shortish man wearing a diamond-encrusted baseball cap backwards, and a fur coat that trailed along the floor like a cape. He wore huge gold glasses with sparkling dollar signs, so big and ridiculous they doubled as a disguise. Around his neck dangled so much bling he could've opened a jewellery store.

The shiny villain flashed a smile that revealed blindingly white teeth with one capped in gold.

'Do you know why I love this place?' he asked loudly. Ethan glanced around the room and saw that everyone was looking down.

'This lovely little establishment doesn't take credit cards. Most of you know who I am, I'm sure ... I am Money Man! So please place all your cash on your tables.'

All the customers did so, including Ethan's parents. Money Man raised his right hand, making a come-here gesture with his index finger, and all the money flew off the tables and into his coat pockets.

Ethan was dumbfounded.

As the cash flowed towards Money Man, the only sound was the scraping of a chair. Everyone turned to look at a man in a green shirt who appeared to be trying to hold himself on his seat.

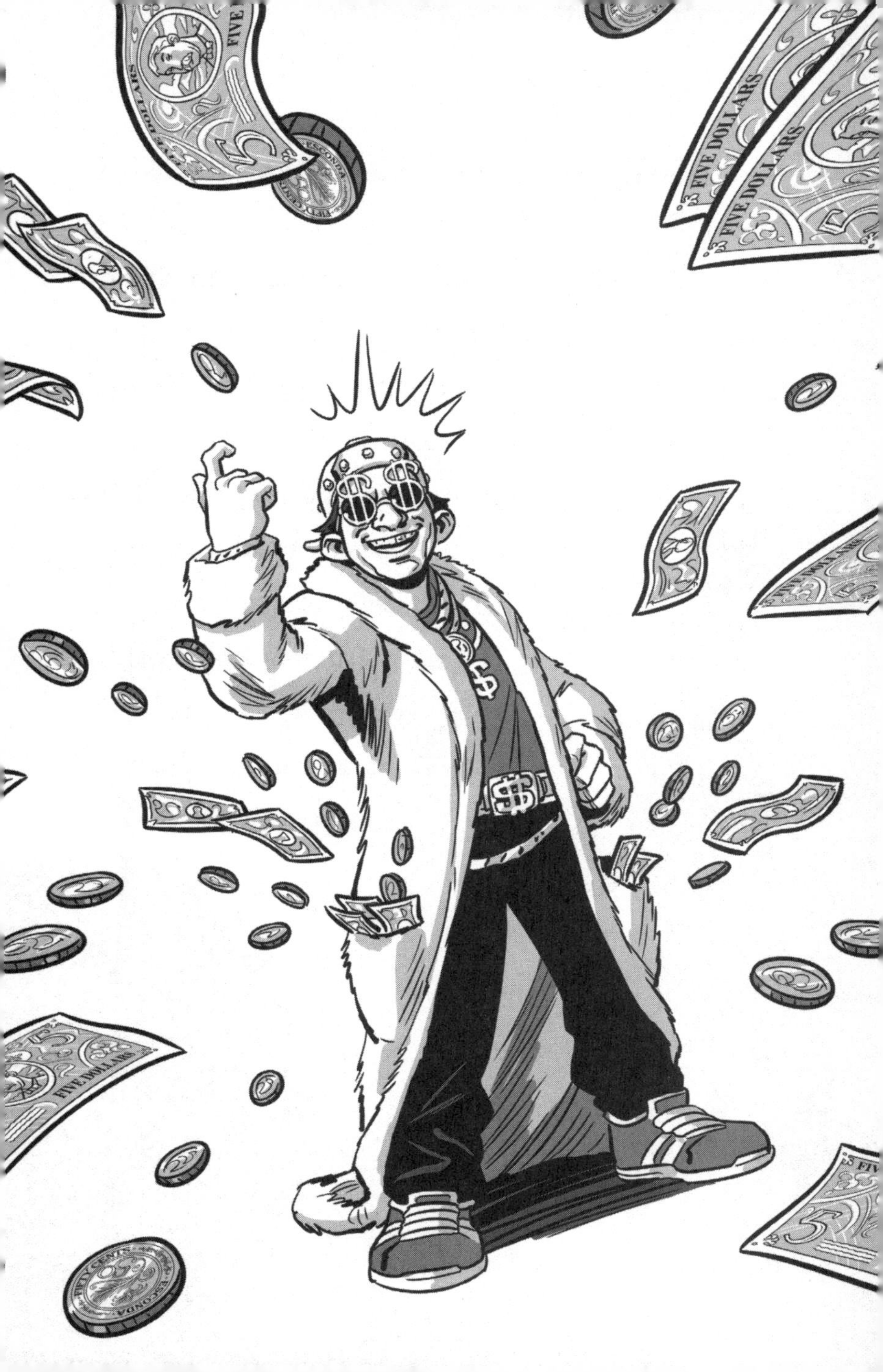
FIVE DOLLARS
FIVE DOLLARS
FIVE DOLLARS

Money Man shook his head. 'There's always one.'

He strolled over to the green-shirted diner. 'What is it?' he asked. 'Two wallets, one to fool thieves and the other with your real funds? Money belt under the clothes?'

Money Man quickly raised his hand, pointing to the ceiling. The diner was flung upwards, and left dangling upside down as if he was being hung by his left foot.

Money Man chuckled. 'In your shoe? Really?' He wriggled his fingers. 'Stuck tight, too. Never mind, it'll just take a bit longer.'

The diner's left foot twitched. Everyone was silent. Ethan realised he was holding his breath.

Suddenly a small ziplock bag full of folded notes flew out of the shoe, and the diner fell in a heap with a worrying thud.

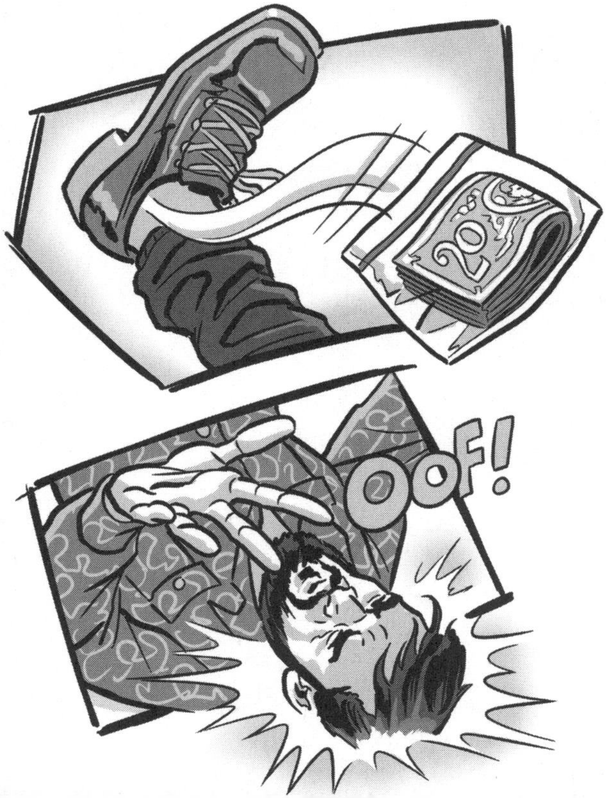

OOF!

An older, tanned man with thinning hair and an apron came out from the kitchen. 'Please, mister,' he said, 'this is the second time this week! I'll have to close!'

Money Man looked at the chef with anger in his eyes.

Fifteen of the smallest coins shot from the fur coat towards the chef. They formed a circle and started to spin, faster and faster, like the blade of a circular saw.

The chef backed away, the coins getting closer and closer to his face. He stopped with his back hard against the wall as the coins drew nearer.

Suddenly the coins stopped in mid-air. Money Man looked thoughtful, then nodded.

'You're right,' he said. 'This could break your business. So . . .'

The smile returned to his face.

NEEAAA

'. . . I better make it worthwhile. Everyone, I'm
going to need you to place all of your jewellery
on the table, or else . . .'

Money Man moved his coin saw to the front
counter and made it spin faster, carving through
the benchtop and sending splinters flying.

Ethan turned to his parents, and watched as each of them put one hand over the other to hide their wedding rings.

Nope, he thought. *I have to do something!*

Ethan sent his thoughts through the restaurant, looking for something he could combat Money Man with. He closed his eyes and saw a flare of silver on the front counter, near where the coins had ripped into the wood. A tablet computer.

Ethan reached out to it. A voice sprang from its speaker, saying, *'Hey you! Yeah you, the idiot in the fur coat and the plastic hat!'*

'PLASTIC?' shouted Money Man. He grabbed the tablet and looked. The metal casing grew warm in his grasp, then with a *BANG* the screen shattered in a flash of light, sending tiny splinters of hard plastic into Money Man's face, cracking his glasses.

'Quick! RUN!' said Ethan. It wasn't just his parents who heard him and leapt up – all the customers stampeded out of the restaurant. In the confusion, Ethan grabbed his backpack from under the table and snuck into the bathroom.

After throwing a jacket over his T-shirt, Ethan put on his E-Boy helmet. He stood in front of the bathroom mirror, looking himself in the eye, and said, 'Here we go again!'

When Ethan stepped back out of the bathroom, Money Man was still looking angrily at his broken glasses and the remnants of the tablet.

Money Man looked up. 'Who are you supposed to be?' he asked. 'Captain Antenna?'

'Never mind who I am. You have to leave.' As he spoke, Ethan searched for more electronics to use, and frowned at the lack of options.

'I guess this was you,' said Money Man, waving at what was left of the tablet. 'You'll pay for that.' He clicked his fingers, and the coin saw started up again. 'EVERYONE PAYS THE MONEY MAN!'

With an almighty crash, the front window of the restaurant shattered inwards as an electric bike veered off the road and flung itself through the window and into the room – towards Money Man's back.

The coins scattered across the floor.

Ethan kept reaching out as Money Man got back to his feet. The coins all stood up on their edges and rolled towards Money Man, who was stretching his back and grimacing. The coins leapt up and started rotating again.

'Was that you?' asked Money Man. 'Not that it matters! I'll—'

A cupboard door flew open and a robot vacuum cleaner sped out.

It cracked into Money Man's ankle, dropping him down again, and then rocketed around the floor, vacuuming up all the coins.

'GIVE THOSE BACK!'

The vacuum stopped and started to shake. Ethan tried to get the vacuum cleaner out of the room, while Money Man willed the coins to burst back out.

Ethan could feel the circuits of the vacuum shorting out and giving way as Money Man shut his eyes to concentrate.

Guess I'll go low-tech, Ethan thought, and picked up a chair, throwing it at Money Man's head while he wasn't looking. Money Man opened his eyes just in time to duck, but his concentration was broken and the vacuum hurried out of the room.

Money Man gave a dog-like growl, and held his fur coat open. The notes he had stolen, plus a lot that he had been carrying, flew out of the coat pockets and rolled up tight. They gathered into two large shapes.

Are they . . . fists?

The left fist swung in fast and Ethan barely managed to get out of its way, moving straight into the path of the right fist.

Ethan shook his head. *That hurt!*

The left fist swung again. Ethan dodged and waited for the right to follow, but instead the left returned with a backhander that sent him staggering.

He reeled close to the bar. Money Man closed in, not content to let the cash fists do their work from a distance. A punch whooshed past Ethan's ear and broke some of the bottles of spirits on display.

Money Man grabbed Ethan by his T-shirt. He pushed hard, bending Ethan backwards over the bar. One of the fists hovered over Money Man's right shoulder, ready to swing. Ethan covered his face with his hands.

Money Man laughed.

Ethan blinked, and the coffee machine behind the bar sent a jet of boiling water straight into Money Man's face. Money Man threw his hands up in time to protect his eyes . . . mostly. Enough steam hit him that he screamed and pulled away.

Ethan searched for another electronic weapon to follow up with while Money Man was hurt – but there was nothing else in the restaurant, there were no more electronic vehicles out in the street, and Money Man wasn't even carrying a phone Ethan could utilise.

There were phones outside, though.

Ethan blinked, and a dozen phones in the street blared with the sound of a police siren.

Still sore and confused, Money Man whipped his head around. He staggered to his feet, headed through the front door and hurried away. The cash fists broke apart, and the money fluttered gently to the floor.

Ethan fought to catch his breath. He felt some of the phones outside being carried back into the restaurant – including his dad's.

He grabbed his backpack and raced into the bathroom again. He pulled off his mask and then found himself fumbling to get his jacket off. Brain still muddled from the fight, it took him a few seconds to realise that his left arm was flopping around uselessly. It felt numb, and he couldn't move it.

'Ethan, are you in here? Are you all right? ETHAN?'

Ethan wrestled the jacket off with one arm, then stumbled back into the restaurant.

Tracy reached him first. 'Oh my goodness, Ethan, are you okay?' she asked as she grabbed him into a hug.

'I'm fine. I just got bumped out of the stampede of people running outside, so I hid in the bathroom. I heard a commotion – what happened?' Ethan hoped his parents wouldn't notice he was only hugging with his right arm.

'We don't know,' said Paul. 'We heard the same noises you did, and saw Money Man run out and away. Are you okay?'

'What's wrong with your arm?' Tracy asked.

'Um . . . I think I hit my shoulder running into the bathroom,' said Ethan. 'It'll be fine. Let's get back to the resort.'

As Ethan climbed into a taxi after his parents, his thoughts were inside his phone. He didn't know exactly where his message was going, but he knew who it was going to.

CHAPTER 4

Agent Ferris had called it 'accommodation', but Penny knew it was a cell.

There were bars on the windows, and an electronic lock. The bed was comfortable but there was no television. The only time she was permitted to use the internet on her laptop, an agent stayed looking over her shoulder.

Penny felt guilty about leaving Ethan, but she needed to be close to Gemini and whatever they were doing with him. Gemini – her life's work, before the government corrupted it – was a doctor, a healer, and Penny believed he could be again. But if the government had their way, he would be an assassin, and to stop that she had to be nearby.

She knew Ethan was hurt and confused, but he was also smart, resourceful and *powerful*. She hoped that sometime she could join him again, but for now—

Penny felt a buzz at her left ankle. When the agents had taken her into custody, even though she'd surrendered and agreed to work with them, they had taken her phone and waved a metal detector over her.

They just hadn't waved low enough.

She had a secret pocket in the cuff of her jeans, and in it was a second phone, a tiny one. It had vibrated as a text message arrived.

Her heart sped up as she read it.

Wherever you are, I need your help. It's urgent. Something has happened to me. I think I'm shutting down. Please help me. Ethan.

Penny went to the window and looked out through the bars, into the night sky.

'Oh no,' she said, 'what's happening to you?'

'She just got a message.'

Two agents, one thin as a ferret, the other a man mountain, sat at a desk covered in screens and communications equipment. One screen showed an alert that a signal had just gone into Penny's cell.

'Who from?' said the bigger agent.

The thin one squinted at his screen. 'Dunno.'

'Okay, *where* is it from?'

The thin agent frowned. 'That's strange, I can't tell that either.'

'That could be . . .' The big agent typed hurriedly, and the largest screen in the room changed from a map to a view of Penny's cell. It showed Penny sitting on the bed holding a phone. The view zoomed in on the hand holding the phone, but the screen was facing away.

Penny stood up, and the view panned back out to show the whole room. She walked to her window. *Oh no, what's happening to you?*

The agents watched as Penny typed a message back, and then stashed her phone back in her jeans cuff.

As the larger man typed, the smaller one said, 'We should be able to see that message.'

The larger man stopped, looking confused.

'We can't. She didn't send it.'

'What?'

'She typed it but didn't send it. There's no signal to intercept.'

'This has to be E-Boy! Wait, what's she doing now?'

Both agents watched as Penny looked around her cell, examining the window and the door.

'She's looking for a way out,' said the bigger man. 'Whatever that message said, she wants to get to the sender.'

'So,' the thin agent said with a smile, 'let's give her a hand.'

For the second time in as many days, Ethan stood at Esconda's international airport, this time to see his parents onto a flight to Switzerland.

The Swiss Alps would be a sharp contrast to Esconda, particularly in temperature, but if that's what it took to make Ethan's parents feel safe again, that's where Ethan would send them.

'I hate to say goodbye to you again so soon, son.' Paul put his hand on Ethan's left shoulder, but Ethan couldn't feel it.

'Are you sure you're okay with us going, Ethan? That arm . . .'

'It'll be fine, Mum,' said Ethan. 'Might just be a week or so before I hit the gym again.'

Ethan's dad chuckled. 'Maybe if you went to a gym at all, you wouldn't have hurt yourself!'

Ethan forced a smile, and after one more half-hug, his parents went through the Customs gate and were gone.

Now that his parents were jetting off to the other side of the world, Ethan felt more alone than ever. Would Penny make it here?

After a night of almost no sleep, Penny still hadn't come up with an escape plan. She knew breakfast was due to arrive in exactly three minutes – they had her on that tight a timetable.

At 7.30 a.m., she heard the buzz and the heavy click of the door opening. An agent came in carrying a tray of grilled mushrooms on sourdough toast.

The food here was always delicious. That was part of the weird relationship between Penny and her captors – because of her expertise, she was a prisoner they were trying very hard to keep happy.

'They're expecting you in the lab in an hour, Doctor,' said the agent. 'Anything you'd like me to tell the technicians?'

As the agent pulled a pen and notepad from inside his jacket, a plain white card, thicker than most, flipped out and landed on the floor.

Penny's breath caught in her throat. *Could that be the keycard for the door?*

'Uh, tell them to have Gemini hooked up to the memory reader,' she said. 'And . . .' She pointed to the nightstand by her bed. 'Could you grab those papers for me?'

The agent turned, and Penny leant down and grabbed the white card from the floor.

'I don't see any papers here, Doctor,' said the agent.

'Sorry, I must've left them in the lab,' said Penny.

'Well, if there's nothing else, I'll be back to escort you to the lab at eight.'

The agent left, the door clunking shut behind him.

Penny dashed to the door and pressed her ear against it, listening to the agent's footsteps heading away. When she couldn't hear them anymore, she studied the card. If her guess was right, it was for a lock that just needed a touch from the keycard. She hoped so, anyway.

Penny pressed the card against the door, and slid it between the door and the wall. *If this is going to work*, she thought, *it's going to be around here . . .*

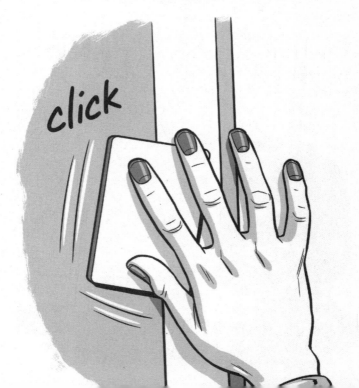

click

She slid the card up and down, hoping –
needing – to trip the magnetic lock. She kept
trying, getting more frantic.

ClicKLUNK

Yes, thought Penny.

Ethan sat in what had been his parents' room at the resort, his eyes closed. His thoughts were inside the computer of Doctor Julius Bao, neurologist. After hours looking up medical information about his arm, a nerve problem seemed most likely, and Doctor Bao was world-famous in the field.

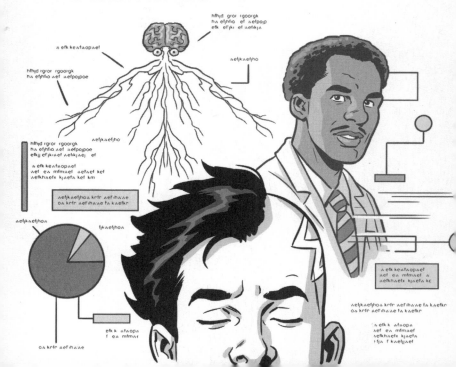

Doctor Bao lived here in Esconda, but people couldn't just walk into his office and ask for his help, even if they could afford it. So Ethan was making fake documents – a referral, a letter of introduction, a boring-looking medical history – directly in Doctor Bao's computer.

He also slotted his name into Doctor Bao's appointments for first thing the next morning.

As Ethan waited in Doctor Bao's office, Penny stepped off the plane from her overnight flight and into Esconda airport. The heat hit her immediately.

For the second night in a row, she had barely slept. She kept waiting for agents to stop her – when she collected the plane ticket that Ethan had arranged, before boarding, before take-off . . . *something*. Even if her escape with the keycard had gone unnoticed by the agents' camera surveillance, surely they'd have found her cell empty by now.

But nothing happened.

She walked across the tarmac, watching as a baggage cart drove past her and her fellow passengers, then stepped through the arrival doors into very welcome air conditioning.

She didn't see the baggage cart pull up beside the plane she had just left, and she didn't see a figure free itself from the bottom of the plane and hide in its shadow before attaching to the side of the cart.

The cart was loaded with luggage. Hidden, Gemini rode it into the terminal.

'It's quite puzzling.'

Doctor Bao was an intense man, younger than Ethan had expected for a world-renowned neurologist. Bao scratched his head through his thick black hair, and frowned.

'You say that you've had no injury to your arm, head or neck?'

'No, not at all,' said Ethan, sitting on the bed in Doctor Bao's examination room.

'Hmmm. There are diseases that affect the nervous system, but nothing that works this quickly. I'll need to run some tests, Mr Forrester . . . I'd like to admit you to our ward at the hospital for a night or two.'

Ethan shrugged. 'If that's what it takes.'

Within twenty minutes, Ethan was in a hospital bed. He was glad to be sitting down, as he was in one of those old-style hospital gowns that doesn't close properly at the back.

He sat connected to different machines, measuring his heartbeat, breathing, brain and muscle activity. He tried to concentrate on the television through the beeping and whirring all around him.

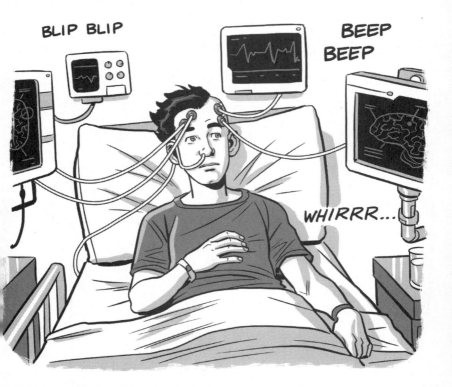

BLIP BLIP

BEEP
BEEP

WHIRRR...

The news was on, running a story about a festival in the nearby city of Aloya – something called Festi Oculta, where the townspeople and tourists were all wearing colourful, elaborate masks.

I wonder if my helmet would qualify, thought Ethan. *That looks fun. I miss fun.*

'The festival highlight is of course the Desfile de Máscaras, the Parade of Masks, featuring colourful floats that the townsfolk have been working on for months. Like every year, it promises to be an amazing party.' The newscaster moved on to the next story. *'And if anyone thought that rumours of Money Man's first failed robbery were going to end his career, a post on his InstaSnap account may change their minds.'*

First failed robbery? Ethan puffed up with pride.

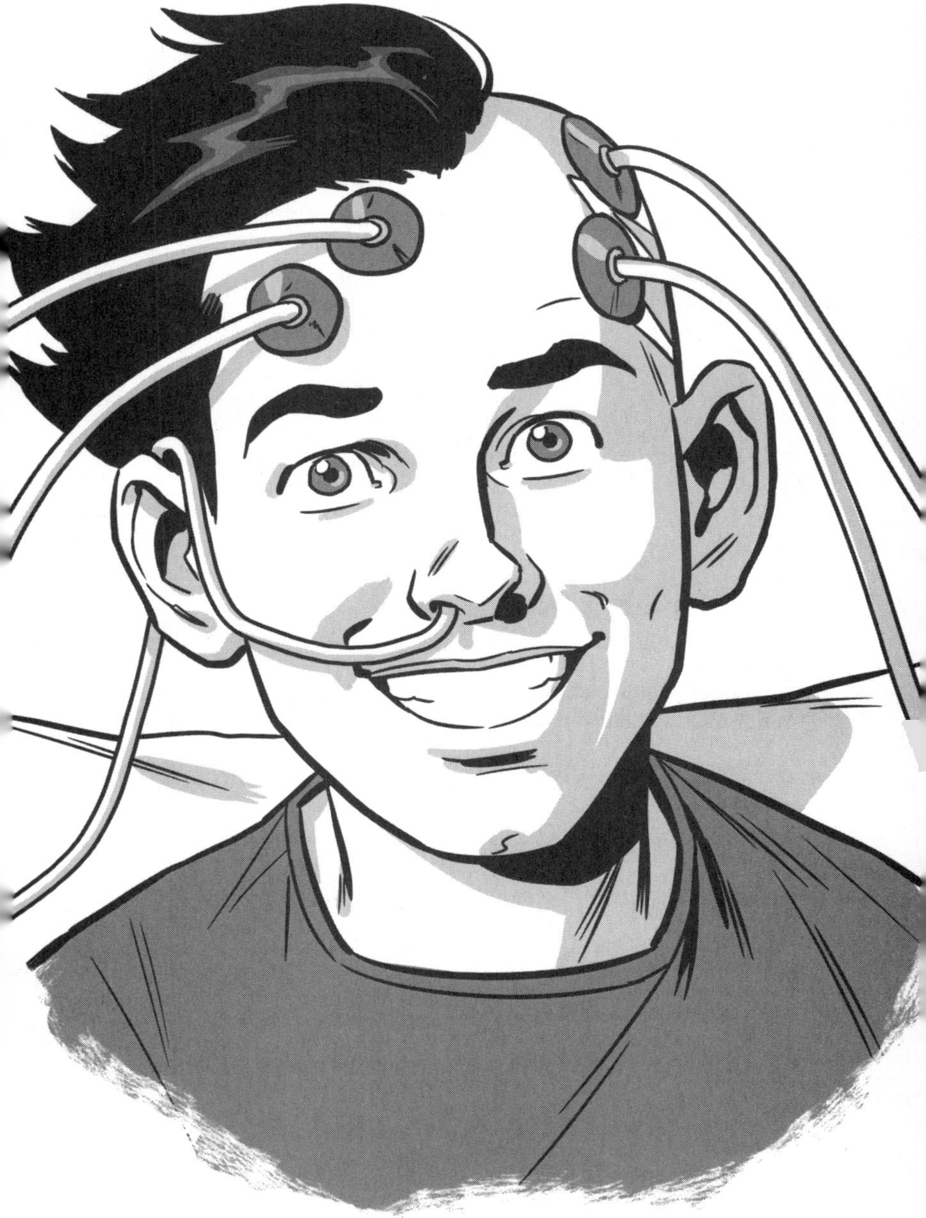

The TV showed a photo of Money Man in a gold bathtub filled with cash, covered in jewellery.

'The post with this photo reads, "Does this look like someone who has failed? Ever? My mansion has more solid gold toilets than I can sit on in a week. Everyone pays the Money Man!"'

Ethan frowned. Before his confrontation with Money Man, his left arm had worked fine. He was in no hurry to see him again.

An elderly woman in a uniform came in, wheeling a drinks trolley, and said something Ethan didn't quite catch.

'Sorry?'

'I was asking if I could get you anything, sweetheart. Cup of tea?'

'No thanks,' replied Ethan.

The old lady gave a sympathetic smile. 'Oh, such a glum face on such a handsome young man. Why are you here?'

Before he knew it, Ethan was telling her about the paralysis in his arm, the mystery about what had caused it, and even how much it had saddened him that he couldn't hug his family properly. He stopped himself there, but something in him longed to open up completely, tell her everything about his powers and his troubles.

What is it about her that makes me want to trust her so much?

The smile vanished from the woman's face, and she leant in close to Ethan's right ear.

'Not all healing happens in a hospital,' she murmured. 'Mysteries are sometimes best cured by the mysterious. There is a man of healing who can fix what those here can't.'

Ethan's eyes opened wide. 'What kind of doctor is he?'

'He's more of a shaman. He lives in the mountains to the east, in a place that can only be reached by boat.'

'How long would it take to get to him?'

'If you are determined enough, you could make the journey in a day. Is your paralysis getting worse? Is it spreading?'

Ethan nodded. 'I think I'm losing the hearing in my left ear.'

'Then go quickly!'

Ethan hesitated. After a moment, the elderly woman put a hand on his shoulder.

'Go while you can,' she said.

Ethan nodded. She smiled, and turned to leave.

'Wait,' said Ethan. 'How will I find him?'

'Follow the river east. He will feel your need, and will find you.'

Ethan unplugged himself from the machines and stood up, immediately feeling the chill of the air conditioning on his bare bum. He dragged his pants on awkwardly, embarrassed.

Once he'd struggled into the rest of his clothes, he quietly slipped out of his room into the corridor.

Before Ethan reached the exit of the hospital building, his phone chimed with an incoming message . . . from Penny!

I've landed. Where are you?

CHAPTER 5

Most of the interest in Esconda centred on the bay – a beautiful harbour filled with million-dollar yachts, leading out to the open ocean.

The river was ignored by most people. It offered less glamour than the bay, and more mosquitos. The taxi driver had given Ethan a weird look when Ethan had told him where to drive, to the only accessible point that wasn't too overgrown or rocky.

Penny arrived a few minutes later, driven by another confused taxi driver. In that time, Ethan had found a lone fisherman, and given him more money than the man could earn in six months of fishing to buy his boat. The fisherman had thrown in a map, which showed just how winding the river was.

Penny dashed up and grabbed Ethan in a fierce hug. 'Ethan, what's wrong, what's happening?'

'I'll explain everything once we're on our way. Hop in the boat and we'll get going.'

'Seriously?' Penny asked.

'A lot of strange things are going on, Penny, but they're all serious.' Ethan pushed a button on the outboard motor and it rumbled into action. 'Please, let's go.'

Penny paused, then nodded and climbed in.

Ethan looked at the map, then turned it upside down. 'Would be so much easier with a GPS!'

As Ethan lowered the propeller into the water and the boat moved away from the shore, neither he nor Penny happened to look back. If they had, they'd have seen a black four-wheel drive with tinted windows drive up.

Gemini stepped out of the car and spotted them, then scanned the area for another boat.

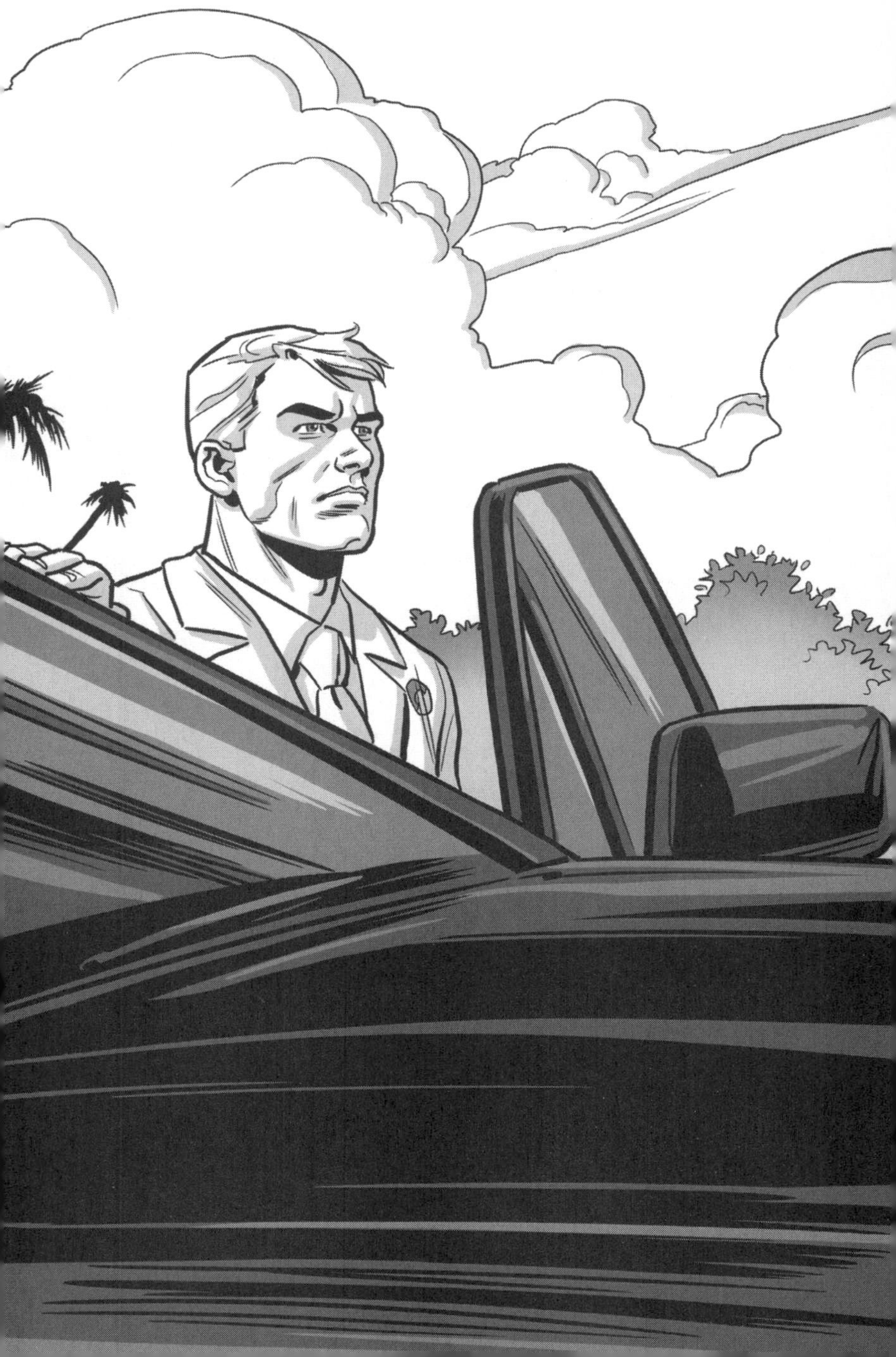

Nothing.

Gemini immediately sprinted towards the river and dived in.

SPLASH

As Penny and Ethan made their way upstream, each told their story. Ethan hadn't told the elderly woman everything, but now the one person he could open up to completely was here. He told Penny about the message from his parents, Money Man, the paralysis, and where they were headed.

'A shaman? *Really?*' said Penny.

Ethan nodded gravely. 'The doctors dunno what's going on, and it's getting worse. So it's great that you got here so fast – how did you get away?'

Penny told Ethan about the dropped keycard, and waiting for a chase that never came.

'They just . . . let you go?'

Penny looked uncertain. 'Well, they . . . uh . . .'

Penny had been grateful for her luck. Now that she told her story out loud, she could hear how unlikely it sounded.

Ethan turned to look behind the boat, saw the wake their vessel was leaving . . . and saw another current in the water, which was getting closer.

'Holy guacamole, Penny, I have a bad feeling that I know why it was so easy,' said Ethan, pointing to the river behind them. 'Look!'

The other current turned into a foamy churn as shapes started to burst through the water. Hands appeared, then full arms, then shoulders and a head.

Penny's eyes were wide with shock. 'Gemini!'

Ethan twisted the throttle on the outboard motor, getting every bit of speed and power out of the engine that he could. The boat pulled away from Gemini a little, but couldn't leave him behind.

Ethan steered the boat towards floating logs and reeds in the river, trying to get Gemini tangled, but the robot avoided them with ease. He started gaining on them.

'There's nothing but trees and rocks and – and *nature* here!' screamed Ethan. 'Nothing electronic for me to use against him!'

'You're more than just your powers, Ethan,' Penny said. 'We'll use our brains.'

As the midday sun beat down, Ethan's good arm started to ache from holding the tiller of the motor. He worried about how much longer the fuel in the engine would last.

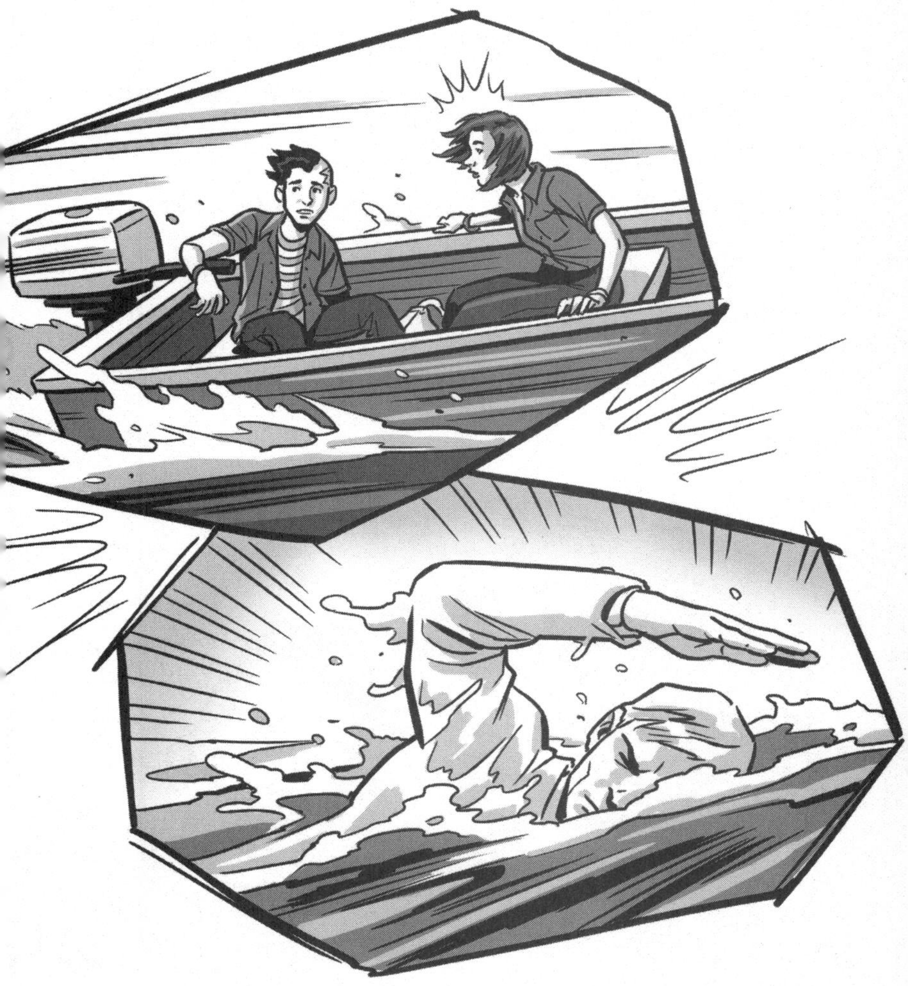

As they kept pushing along the river, they saw a junction ahead. The way upstream continued to the left, while another downstream path split off to the right.

They could hear a faint rushing sound. Penny looked at the map.

'Ethan, there's a problem. If we keep going upstream, there's no way we can keep our speed up. He'll catch us.'

'What's to the right?'

'Three sharp turns, then a waterfall.'

The colour drained from Ethan's face. 'Then we're trapped.'

A few seconds passed. Then Penny said, 'I have a crazy idea.'

'Crazy is better than none!'

'Turn the boat off to the right.'

Ethan's eyes grew large. 'Towards the waterfall?!'

Penny shrugged. 'I said it was crazy!'

At the junction, Ethan hauled on the tiller and sent the boat downstream.

The river bent tightly, too tightly to see where Gemini was. Penny craned her neck and looked up, then stood in a crouch.

Ethan tried not to panic. 'What are you doing?!'

'Do you need me to say the "crazy" thing again?' Penny bent down and grabbed the anchor that lay in the bottom of the boat. 'Put your backpack on!'

Ethan did as she said, and they rounded the final bend before the waterfall. The sound of water rushing over the rocks ahead of them filled their ears.

Ethan felt his heart thumping through his chest. He glanced at Penny, who was looking up. He turned to the back of the boat, just as Gemini came into view.

'PENNY!' he shouted.

'GRAB ME!' she screamed back, as she hauled
the anchor up and threw it into the air.

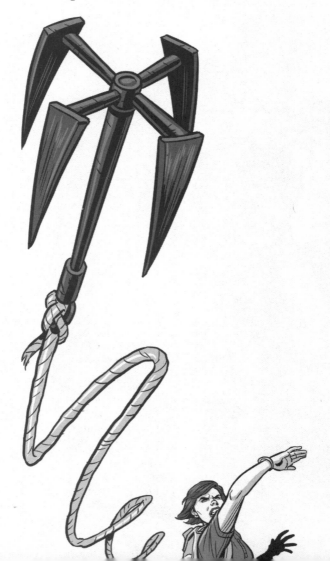

The anchor flew up into an overhanging tree and snagged on a branch. Penny grabbed the rope that dangled from it and Ethan lunged at her, grabbing her pack as the boat sped out from underneath them and over the waterfall's edge.

Penny gave a half-grunt, half-cry as she took Ethan's weight.

Gemini tried to adjust his path as the current took him. He thrashed upwards and grabbed for Ethan's foot, just missing it!

Gemini turned in the water and tried to swim against the current, but even his robotic strength wasn't enough. The river took him over the falls.

'Arrrrrgggghhhhh!!' shouted Ethan.

'I NEED YOU TO CLIMB!' replied Penny.

They both hauled themselves up onto the branch, holding the anchor.

Gemini dangled by one arm and looked back up through the water to the top of the waterfall. *Distance: 75.3 metres.*

He looked down. *Distance: 32.4 metres.*

He scanned for other handholds as the water cascaded around him. *None available.*

Solution – make some.

Gemini curved the fingers of his free arm into a hook, and cracked them into a rock. And again. And again.

CRACK!
CRACK!
CRACK!

By his fourth strike, the fingers had created enough of an opening to hold onto. He pulled himself up and started to repeat the process. *Caa-RACK. Caa-RACK.*

Ethan and Penny pushed their way through the jungle.

Ethan almost lost a shoe in the mud when a thought struck him. 'Penny, if Gemini survived that fall, he's coming after us, right?'

'Yeah. He won't stop. If someone's given him a directive, he can't stop.'

'He'll look for footprints.' Ethan pulled a couple of vines free, sat down and took his shoes off. 'Let's make things a bit tricky.' He used the vines to tie his shoes backwards to his feet.

Penny nodded and did the same.

They wound their way through more jungle, leaving backwards footprints, and eventually made their way back to the river. There was a stretch of riverbank covered in smooth stones. Ethan untied his shoes from his feet and slung them around his neck, walking along the stones barefoot.

'This is clever,' said Penny. 'It worries me a little. You're starting to think like a fugitive.'

'Well, we've been running a while now,' said Ethan.

Penny untied her shoes and followed. Ethan pulled the map from his back pocket and opened it up.

'I tell you, when I do stop running, I'm never going anywhere without GPS signal. Using a big piece of paper like this is driving me nuts.'

Gemini reached the top of the waterfall and scanned for signs of his targets. The anchor and rope they used to escape were gone, but Gemini still knew which tree they had climbed.

What for most people would involve a lot of careful thought and analysis, Gemini processed in an instant.

Targets were heading along the river.

Targets turned this way to send me towards the waterfall to evade capture.

Targets were headed upstream before turning this way – conclusion: targets' goal is further upstream.

Strategy: continue upstream.

Gemini started swimming.

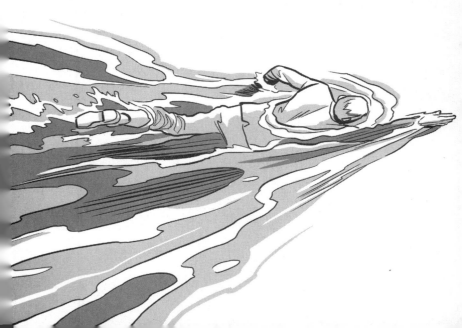

Further along the river, a jetty stuck out into the water. Ethan and Penny looked at each other; the sudden nature of their escape meant they had lost their supplies to the waterfall, and they were starving. A jetty might mean a nearby village – and food.

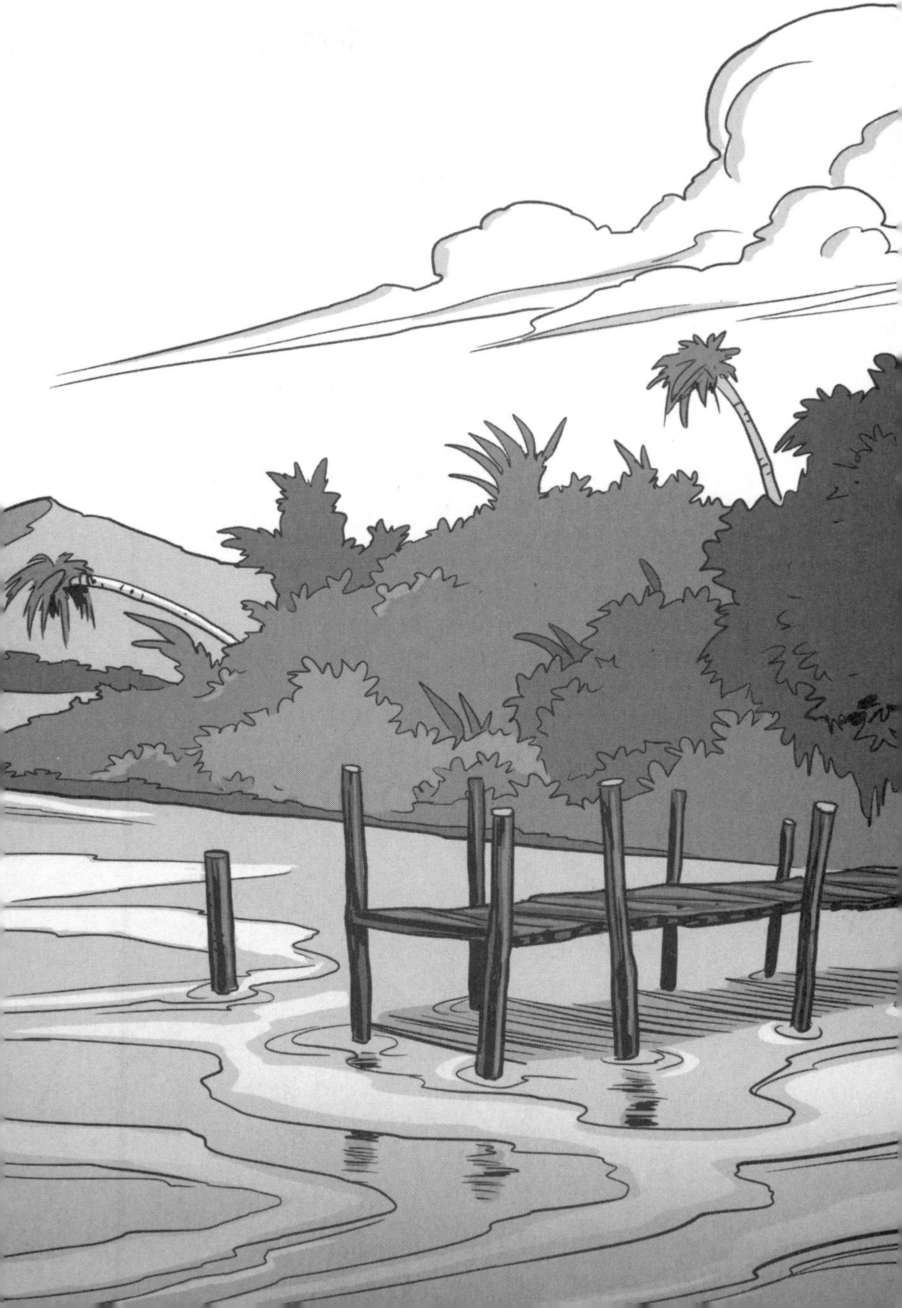

A path ran from the jetty through the jungle. It led them to a village of thatched huts and houses.

Ethan ran from doorway to doorway, while Penny stopped to survey the scene.

'Hello?' said Ethan. 'Is anybody here? Can you help us? Hello?'

'Ethan . . .' Penny said gently.

When Ethan replied, his voice held a mixture of disappointment and panic. 'There's no one here. There's nothing here.'

'Ethan, look around,' said Penny.

Ethan stopped running and looked around. There was ash along the ground. One section of trees was charred and blackened, not a spot of green. The plants either side were wilted and dead.

'What happened?' said Ethan.

'I'm not sure. Listen – there are no sounds of wildlife. Whatever did this, it was big, and it made this village unliveable.'

Ethan sighed. 'Well then, this place is a bust. We need to get back on track.' He unfolded the map. 'If we head due west, we can meet up with the river again,' he said, pointing up on the map.

'That's north,' said Penny.

'Are you sure?' replied Ethan.

'Yep. On any map like this, north is always up.'

'Oh sure. Of course. I knew that. North gets us back to the river.'

Ethan looked at the compass hanging around his neck, then headed north. Penny gave him a worried look as she followed.

Gemini swam. The current seemed to drag on his right side, but he could compensate for that easily. Soon he spotted a freshly broken branch onshore.

Possible human movement, he thought.

He climbed onto the bank and looked near the branch, finding footprints pointing away from the river.

He followed them for a few metres, then discovered one in slightly deeper mud than the rest. The mud had shifted strangely, as if the person walking had stepped with their toe landing first, then the heel.

That is not how people walk.

Gemini crouched, then dug the fingers of his left hand into the ground to lift some of the print up to analyse it. When he lifted his hand, though, a lot more dirt came up than he expected, much faster than he intended, destroying the footprint completely.

He stopped. *Possible sensory damage from waterfall.*

He looked at the next footprint, which had the same strange mud pattern, and dug his right hand in to retrieve some. This time it came as expected, no extra dirt or speed in the movement.

Difference in readings between left and right hands/ arms, he thought.

He looked at the part-footprint in his hand. This person had definitely been walking toe-first . . .

Or has reversed their footwear to make the prints appear to originate from the river, whereas they actually run to it.

Gemini turned around to head back to the riverbank, then stopped. He picked up a dead branch with his right hand, then put it down. He picked it up again, this time with his left, and snapped it in half without meaning to.

Left hand/arm stronger than right. Noted for future action/movement. Stronger left arm may explain earlier feeling of the river dragging on right side.

Gemini returned to the river and resumed swimming.

The sun sank lower in the sky. Ethan and Penny were tired and hungry, but they pressed on through the jungle. They suddenly came to a sheer rockface that went up for at least twenty metres, and Ethan nearly fainted.

'There's no way I can climb that,' he protested. 'This has all been for nothing! I was in a perfectly good hospital, why did I listen to—'

'This way,' said Penny. Around the curve of the cliff she had found an opening, a crack just wide enough for them to shuffle through sideways.

Ethan didn't say anything, just stood there with an embarrassed look on his face.

'Don't worry about it,' said Penny. 'This has been rough, and we're both exhausted. We've come this far, though. Let's keep going.'

Ethan nodded and stepped into the opening.

They sidled their way through. Ethan thought of his arm. *The only muscles that aren't aching are the ones I can't feel at all.*

As the sun dipped closer to setting, the path grew darker until one side opened up – completely. Where they had been between two rockfaces, now they were on a thin ledge near a forty-metre drop.

They eased forwards, their backs brushing against the rockface behind them, sending tiny pebbles plummeting down. Ethan closed his eyes, inching forwards by feel, until he heard a loud *CRUNCH!* He opened his eyes and saw a spear, shuddering in the rock, pinning his shirt to the cliff!

'ETHAN!' shouted Penny. Another *CRUNCH*, and a spear had caught Penny's collar and pinned her to the rockface too.

Ethan looked straight ahead and saw the blur of four more spears coming at them. He shut his eyes tight and heard *CRUNCH CRUNCH CRUNCH CRUNCH*, sticking more of his and Penny's clothes to the rock.

After a few seconds of silence Ethan dared to open his eyes again. In the dimming light, he could make out the figures of about twenty people, most of them still holding spears.

'What do they want? What *could* they want?!' said Penny.

'We're not in a great spot to run,' said Ethan, 'so I guess we'll find out.'

CHAPTER 6

Just as the sun was setting, Ethan and Penny were led into a village that looked like the abandoned one they had found earlier, except here firepits shone and flickered with flames, and people walked in and out of the thatched huts.

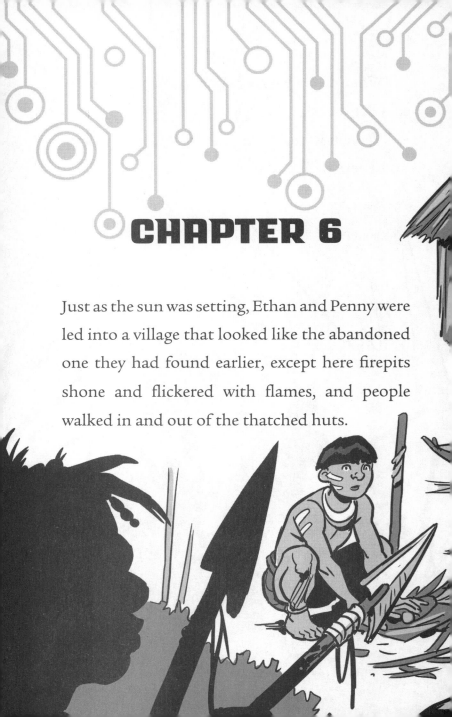

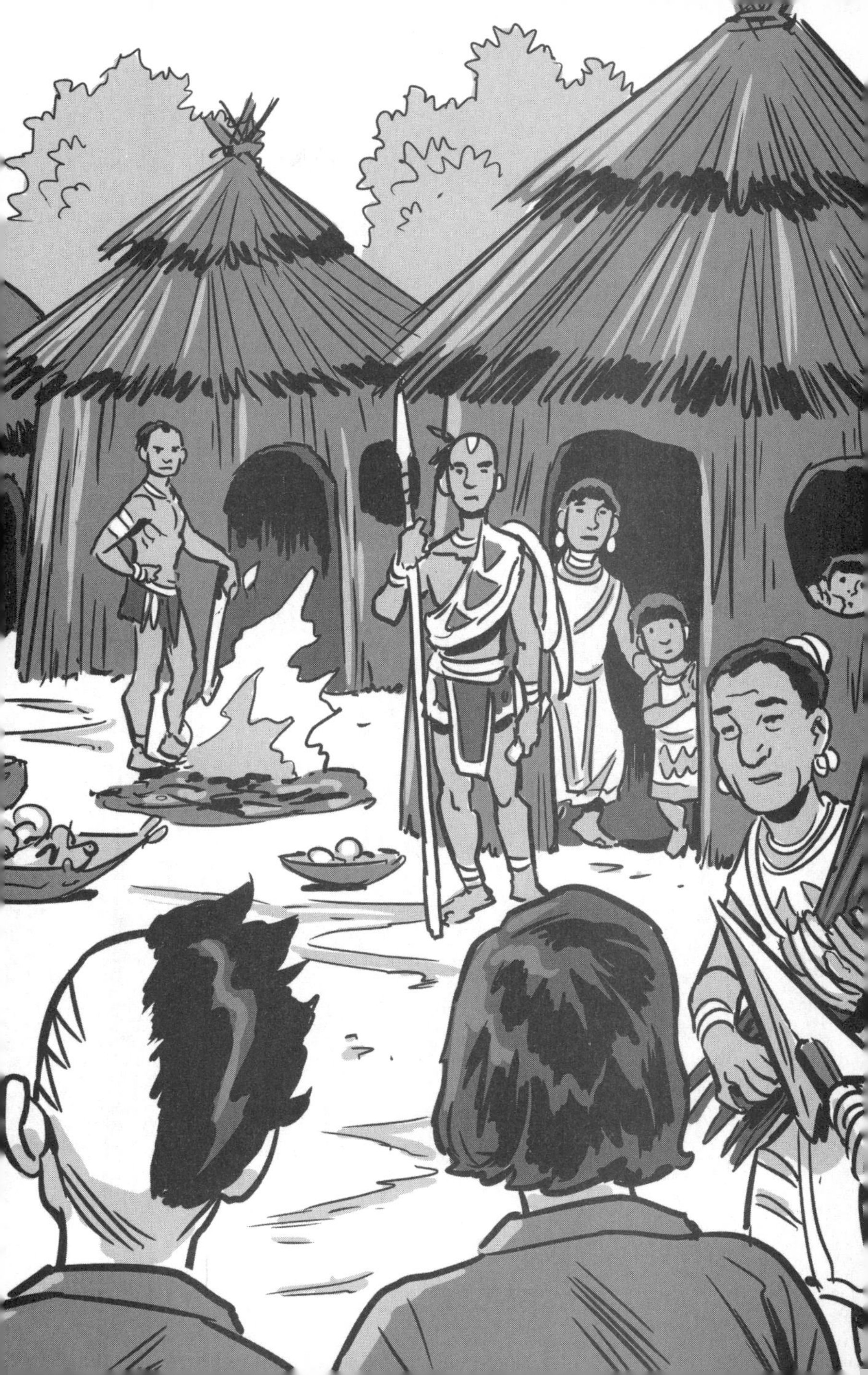

Ethan was exhausted, and one look at Penny told him she was too. Their captors had given them water, and were now half-leading, half-dragging them forwards by the vines tied around their wrists. Eventually they were brought before a huge chair carved out of a massive tree trunk – the only chair of any kind they could see.

The group that had found Ethan and Penny started clapping in a slow rhythm, a mixture of loud and soft. *CLAPclapCLAPCLAPclapCLAP-CLAPclapCLAPclapCLAPCLAPclapCLAPCLAP-clap.*

The clapping sped up until it seemed to fill the entire jungle. Penny looked around nervously – Ethan no longer had the energy to be scared.

The clapping stopped abruptly as a bald man stepped into view, wearing a cloak of brightly coloured feathers. He climbed the stairs up to the wooden throne.

More warriors carrying spears joined the first group until they formed a complete circle around their captives and their leader.

The bald man gazed at Ethan and Penny silently, no expression on his face. After a few minutes he said, 'Why have you come here?'

Ethan stood as upright as he could and took a step forwards. He told the chief of his paralysis and its spread, and how an elderly woman in the hospital in the city told him of a shaman in the eastern mountains who could help.

The bald man smirked. 'You make such a difficult journey on the say-so of one old woman?'

Ethan gave a one-shouldered shrug. 'Yeah, I was just saying that to myself a couple of hours ago.'

The bald man laughed. 'You were expecting to find a wise old man, yes? Someone who has learnt much over a long life, and can use long-forgotten knowledge to heal you where others have failed?'

Before Ethan could reply, the man continued. 'We have no shaman here. We have had no shaman in this village for as long as I have been alive.'

Ethan felt his knees buckle and threaten to give way completely.

The bald man kept talking. 'We do, however, have a Charlemayne, who may be able to help. You have arrived just in time, as he does not take

visitors late into the evening. Do not seek too much from him tonight, though – he has already had his milk, and if kept up past his bedtime he gets cranky.'

Ethan stood, trying to make sense of the bald man's words.

'Charlemayne, join us, please.'

A gap formed in the circle of warriors, and a small boy stepped into the group. At least he *seemed* to be a small boy – Ethan looked into his eyes and saw something deep, something old. Something calm.

Charlemayne walked up to Ethan, walked around him. Ethan watched as the boy got closer and looked him in the eye. Charlemayne ran a hand up Ethan's paralysed arm – Ethan didn't feel anything, but the boy winced.

Charlemayne took Ethan's left hand and closed his eyes. Ethan thought he felt a tingle, but that might have been hope rather than any change in the arm itself.

Charlemayne's eyes opened, but he wasn't looking at Ethan – or anyone in particular. He spoke in a voice that didn't seem to belong to a child. 'They start as two, but joined as one by a storm. Now one grows dimmer while the other brightens. One is here, the other—'

The boy stopped suddenly, then looked around frantically. He ran to the throne and grabbed the bald man's leg. Charlemayne pointed back out to the jungle, at the path that Ethan and Penny had walked in on.

In an instant, Charlemayne had gone from a source of mystery and wonder to a frightened child.

From the throne, the bald man boomed. 'Who else has come with you? Who have you brought to our village?!'

Penny stepped forwards. 'I'm sorry – we didn't mean to bring anyone else, but someone is following us,' she said. 'We have tried to shake him off, but we may not have been successful.'

The bald man stood up. 'Charlemayne would not be reacting so badly if this person wasn't a dire threat!'

'He isn't . . . I mean, he is a threat, he isn't a . . . person, really,' Penny stammered. 'We need your help.'

Gemini wasn't worried about the setting sun. With his advanced sensors, he wouldn't miss daylight much.

Gemini found the same jetty that Ethan and Penny had, and followed their footprints – the right way around this time – to the abandoned village, and out again. As the last of the sunset disappeared, he kept on their trail to the north.

Gemini edged his way along the same tight cliff path, finding six divots in the rockface that had tiny fragments of cloth in them. He looked closer.

Cloth identical to clothes worn by targets.

As he stepped onto easier ground, his sensors started to detect smoke wafting through the air around him. At first it was just a wisp, but soon it grew thick. Gemini engaged sonar, sending out soundwaves and learning about his surroundings by how long they took to bounce back, just like a bat. But that didn't give him the kind of detail he needed to continue tracking Ethan and Penny.

Gemini crouched on all fours, and found the footprints again. Staying low, he followed them through the jungle, but they seemed to be following strange patterns – turning suddenly when there was no obstacle to going straight ahead, curving back on themselves . . .

Gemini saw three rocks at the base of a tree, and realised he had been past them before. But the footprints were different this time. He stopped, and stood.

Trail appears to be changing. Possible system failure, linked to issues with left arm?

As Gemini experienced his version of doubt, a shoe flew by him through the smoke.

He calculated where the shoe had been thrown from, walked towards that spot, and crouched again. Footprints crisscrossed in different directions. Nearby, the quick rhythm of a person running zipped past him. He moved to follow, but stopped when another shoe . . . or maybe the same one . . . sped past his face.

This time he walked in the direction the shoe was moving. He looked down, and saw footprints appear apparently from nowhere. He followed them for a few steps, then through a gap in the smoke saw two shoes – Ethan's shoes – on feet that were running away.

He followed, the smoke thinning, the sprinter losing more of his lead with each step.

The chase quickened. Gemini watched as the shoes leapt over branches and around trees. Gemini sped up and got within arm's reach to grab his prey, spinning him around to see . . .

It wasn't Ethan.

'Where is the owner of those shoes?' said Gemini.

'I don't know,' said the tribesman.

Gemini looked at his captive. *Signs of stress, faster heartbeat. He could be lying, or just frightened.*

Gemini grabbed the man with his left hand, and the tribesman yelped in pain. *Left arm appears to be growing stronger still. Adjusting.*

'TELL ME WHERE HE IS,' Gemini shouted.

'I don't know. The chief deliberately didn't tell us where he was going, just in case we got caught!'

Gemini paused for a split second, then said, 'Take me to your village.'

Penny led Ethan through the darkness of the jungle, each wearing sandals that the chief had given them. They had also been given a small pack of food, half of which they had wolfed down immediately, and two water bottles.

'I need to stop,' Ethan gasped. 'Just need to sit for a sec.'

Ethan sat down with a thud at the base of a tree. Penny looked around, but there was no sign of pursuit at the moment, so she sat next to him.

Ethan's breathing returned to normal. 'What was that kid talking about? One grows dimmer while the other brightens? Is that dimming one supposed to be me? What's going on?'

Penny looked down at her feet.

'Penny? Do you know something?'

Penny breathed in deeply. 'I don't know for certain, but I have an idea of what he might have meant.'

'What is it?' asked Ethan. 'Those words have been bouncing around my head for hours!'

Penny sighed. 'He said "joined as one by a storm". That lightning that struck the hospital while Gemini was operating on you – I think it did more than give you your powers and Gemini his extra thoughts. I think it connected you both. Your powers came from taking a bit of his electronic being, while his . . . emotions, I guess, came from your humanity. Joined by the storm.'

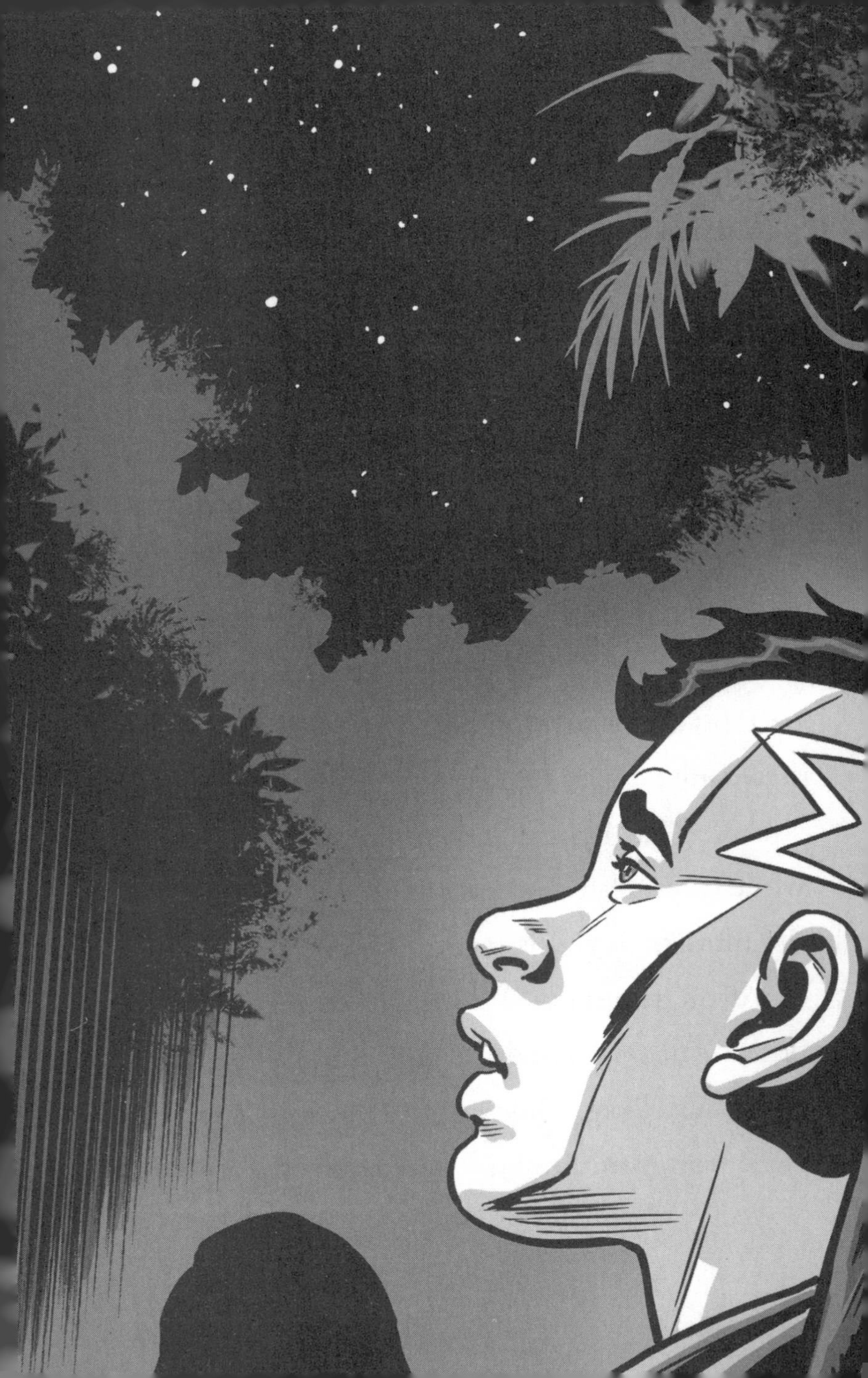

Ethan rested his head back against the tree and looked at the stars through a gap in the jungle foliage. 'So I am the one growing dimmer.'

Gosh, this is so much to take in, Ethan thought.

He turned to Penny. 'Gemini's growing brighter? That means he's getting stronger as I get weaker, right?'

Penny nodded. 'I think so. Are your powers getting weaker too, or just your body?'

Ethan looked at her fiercely. '*Just* my body?!'

'Keep your voice down!' said Penny. 'I'm sorry, that sounded bad, but you know what I mean.'

'I haven't used my powers for a couple of days, so I don't really know. Could Gemini take my power too?!'

Penny bit her lip. 'I'm not sure, but it's what I'm afraid of.'

Ethan ran his right hand through his hair. Tears started to form in his eyes. 'What am I gonna do?'

Penny put a hand on his shoulder. 'I have an idea. There's one woman whose work I've been following – biology and robotics. She's working on making artificial limbs that actually feel, and—'

'I want to get my arm working again, not replace it!' snapped Ethan.

Penny just gazed at Ethan until he calmed down. *I forget that he's so young to be going through all this. I must be more careful.* 'What I meant was, she knows more than anyone on the planet about electronics and human tissue working together. If anyone can help you, it's her.'

Ethan's shoulders slumped. 'So where is she? Middle of the desert? Bottom of the ocean? The moon?'

'Bombara. Not the other side of the world, but we'll still need an airport.'

Ethan shrugged and said, 'So where's the nearest airport?'

Penny unfolded the map, and tilted it towards the moonlight. 'There's a small airfield in Aloya.'

'What do I remember that name from?' Ethan pinched the bridge of his nose. 'The thing with masks . . . what was it called . . .'

'Festi Oculta. Everyone wears a mask. It's world-famous.'

'Well,' said Ethan, 'that'll make it easier to hide.' He stood up. 'Look, I'm sorry I said that stuff. It just – it just gets hard. You know.'

'I know it does,' said Penny, wrapping Ethan in a hug.

'There's another bit of good news,' Penny said, leading Ethan further along the track.

'What's that?' asked Ethan.

Penny pushed away a lush branch to reveal that they were back at the river. Tied to a log at the water's edge was a canoe, big enough for two people.

'Aloya is downstream from here,' said Penny.

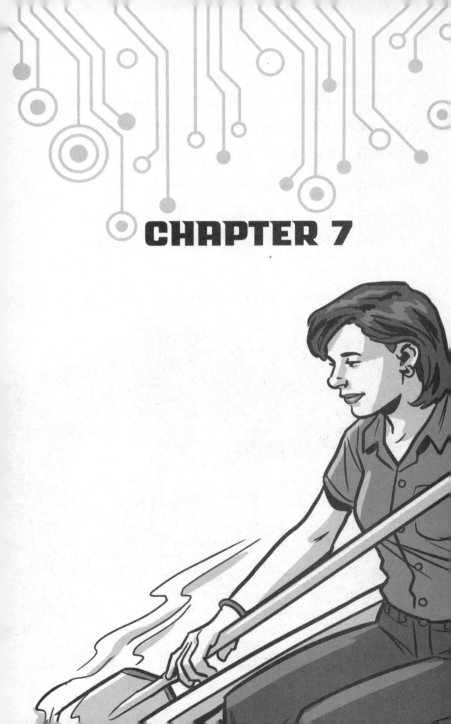

CHAPTER 7

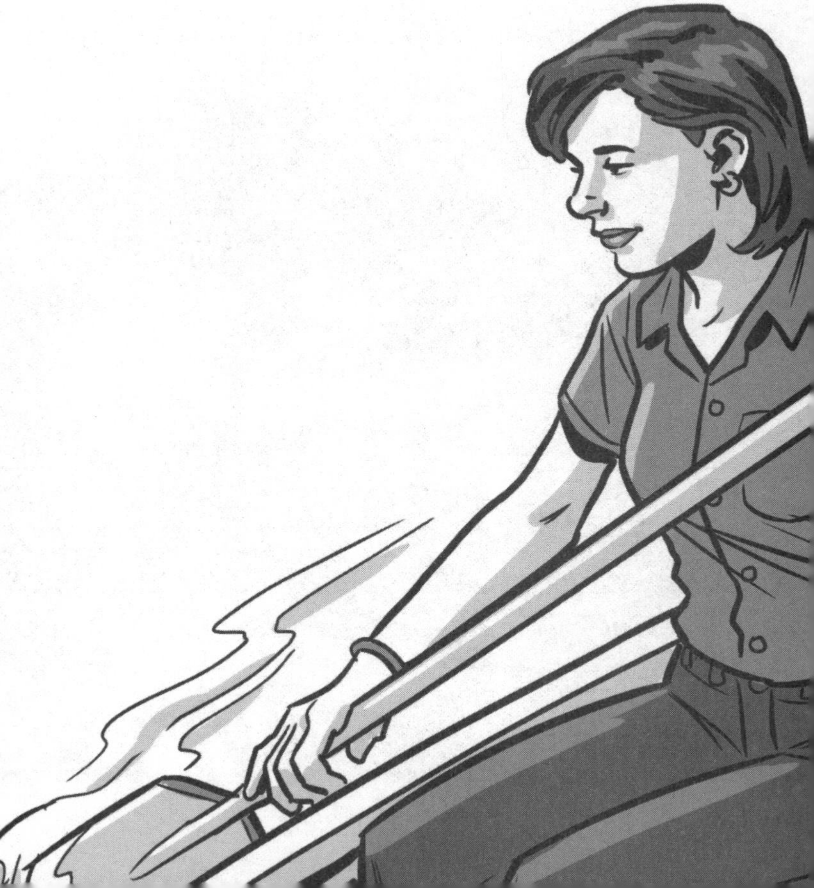

Ethan and Penny spent about a day and a half gliding downstream along the river. The tribal chief had given them food and water, and the trip was mainly uneventful.

Twice they had to carry the canoe around rocks and rapids, and once they had to paddle hard to avoid going back towards the waterfall, but for most of the journey they could relax and recharge.

As they came closer to Aloya, they could hear the festival long before they could see it. The drums sounded like an excited heartbeat, and they could hear happy voices cheering and singing. Ethan sat up straight, feeling energised for the first time in days.

Ethan noticed that Penny was looking at him. 'What?' he asked.

'You're smiling. It's nice to see,' said Penny, smiling back.

They guided the canoe to a sheltered section of the bank, about a hundred metres away from the main jetty, so they could make a sneakier entrance.

It wasn't long before they were walking along
a road – a proper, sealed road for the first time
in what felt like forever – and heading into the
bustle. As they reached the town, they saw people

dressed every which way. Some were in tuxedos
and evening gowns, some in suits and dresses, all
the way to swimwear and thongs. But whatever
their outfit, every single person was wearing a
mask.

Penny saw a street vendor nearby with a big sign on his cart. *MASCARAS – MASKS*

She grabbed Ethan's hand and took him over, pulling out her wallet. 'Two, please. *Dos.*'

'I didn't know you spoke Spanish,' said Ethan.

'I don't,' replied Penny. 'That and *gracias* are pretty much all I have.'

The vendor reached under the cart and brought up two masks – a pig and a poodle.

Ethan and Penny looked at the masks, and each other.

'I don't think I want to be either of those!' said Ethan.

The vendor shrugged. 'I am most sorry, but this is day three of the festival. These are the only *mascaras* I have left.'

Penny paid the vendor, said, *'Gracias,'* and put the poodle mask on straight away, with a cheeky smile.

Ethan frowned and picked up the pig mask. He struggled to put it on one-handed.

Penny's smile vanished. 'Here, let me help.'

'I can do it.' Ethan pulled it on, and felt awkward. Then he looked around at all the masked partygoers singing, chatting and grinning. *Hiding my face out in the open is actually kinda nice.* He puffed up his chest and said, 'How do I look?'

'You know, you look just like Agent Ferris!'
Penny said, and they both laughed.

A few metres away was a bus stop, with a full map of the town. On the far left-hand side of the map was a big red dot, with the words *YOU ARE HERE*. On the far right was an arrow, and *TO ALOYA AIRFIELD*.

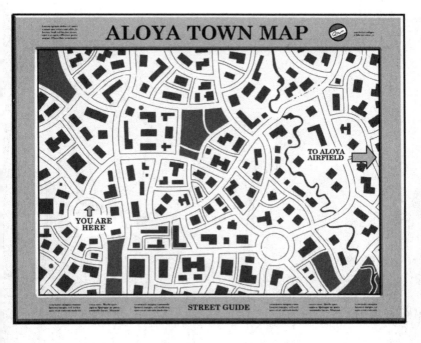

'Looks like we have to get all the way across town, through the party,' said Ethan.

'It'll be slow going, but it could be fun,' said Penny.

'Sure,' said Ethan, trying not to give away how tired he felt. 'Stay on my right side, though. I won't be able to hear you talk through my left ear.'

Penny nodded. 'Let's go.'

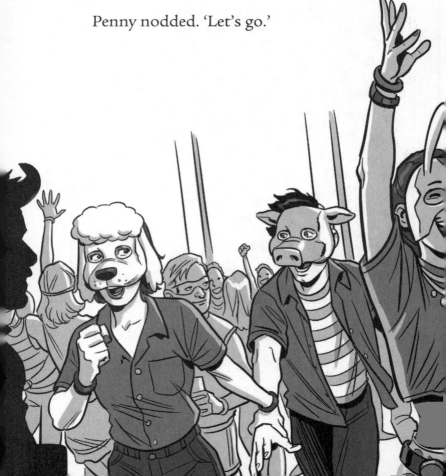

As they walked past a phone shop, Penny stopped. 'Of course, we'll be back in mobile phone range – Ethan, try to use your powers, see how strong they feel.'

Ethan looked at a smartphone on display in the window, a demonstration video showing on its screen. He closed his eyes and reached out along the mobile network. He was used to streams of silver spreading out before his thoughts, offering him anywhere and everywhere in cyberspace that he wanted to go.

This time was different.

Instead of streams he saw thin threads, occasionally broken. There were large patches of darkness. He wasn't wearing his helmet, and Aloya might not have the best network, but this was worrying.

Ethan concentrated harder and the silver strands grew brighter and thicker for a moment. He let them fade again – he didn't want another nosebleed like at the Robofight Games.

'Are you okay, Ethan?'

Ethan opened his eyes and saw Penny looking concerned.

'I'm fine. My powers seem a bit weaker than usual . . . I'm probably just a bit tired and out of practice.'

Penny smiled and said, 'Sure,' but her eyes showed her doubts.

They started weaving through the crowd until it got too thick to pass through.

'This road is blocked,' said Penny. 'There's some sort of barrier that everyone's standing at.'

Ethan remembered the news report he'd seen back in the hospital. 'There's a parade. They've probably got the route fenced off.'

The partygoers ahead started to cheer and clap. Ethan and Penny managed to push their way through to the barrier and saw the first float – a giant masquerade mask made from enormous red and black feathers. The rest of the float was a stage, on which four masked dancers whirled and kicked in time with the drumbeat that seemed to be everywhere through the streets.

The dancers smiled and waved at the crowd . . . until the float lurched to the right, then the back kicked up like a rodeo horse trying to buck its rider. The smiles left the dancers' faces as they grabbed onto the poles to stop themselves falling off.

The float stopped moving forwards and slowly started to tip sideways. People screamed. The dancers jumped and scrambled to get off. When the float came to rest on its side, everyone could see what had caused the problem.

A growing pile of cash.

RUMBLE RUMBLE

The crowd looked at the strange pile of money. Some had an idea of what it may mean, but hoped they were wrong.

The cash started to lift off the ground, note by note, swirling until it formed a tornado. Dust kicked up and obscured the crowd's view, getting in the eyes of the closest spectators.

The drums stopped.

The whole street fell silent, except for the wind made by the money tornado.

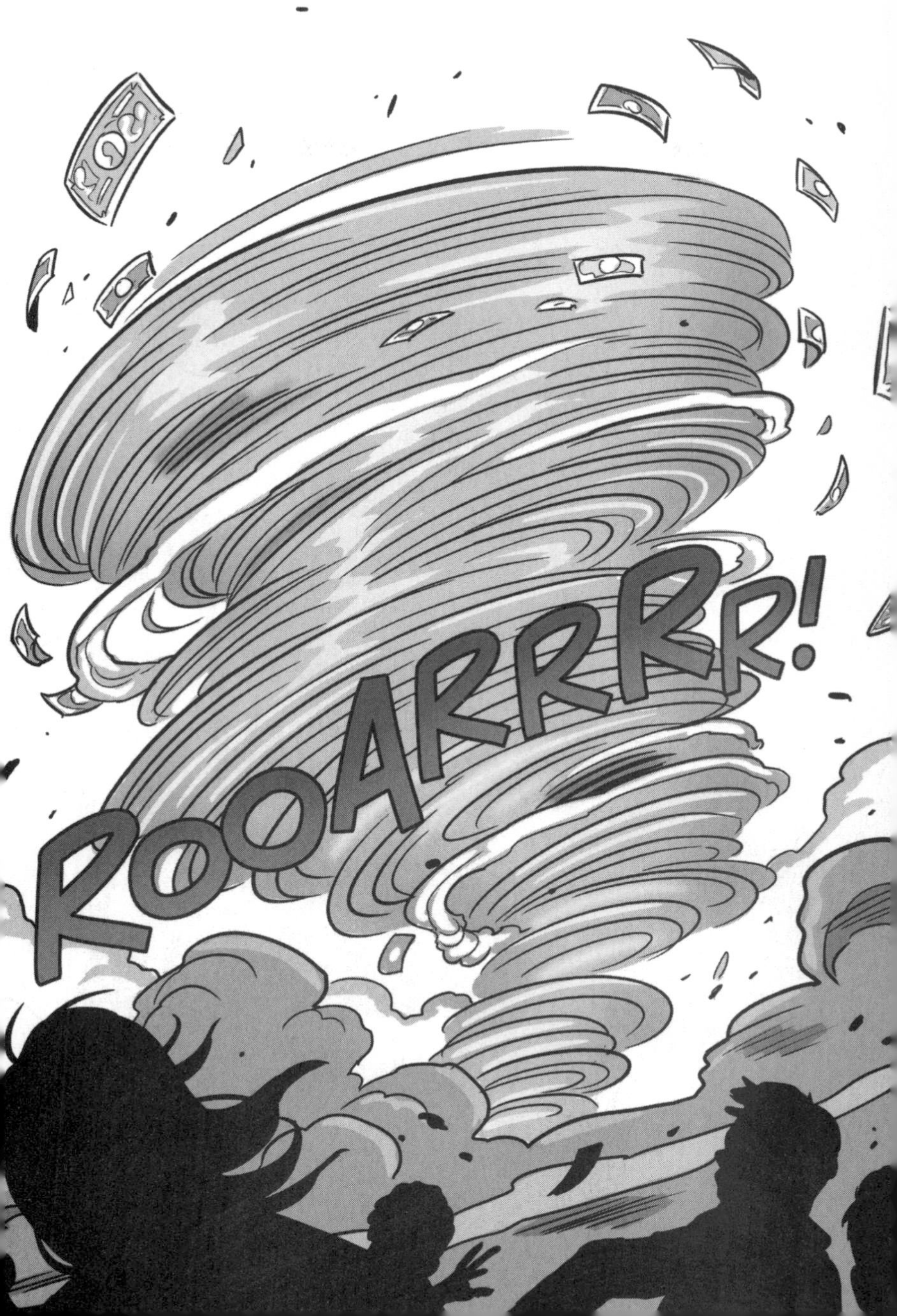
ROOARRRR!

Suddenly the cash disappeared, leaving only the dust cloud.

Until . . .

It looked like a warped version of the first float. Instead of the masquerade mask, there was a giant pair of glasses with dollar signs where the lenses should be, made entirely of gold coins. More coins made the wheels, and the poles. The canopy, and the rest of the float, was formed from tightly packed notes.

Standing on the stage, in a leopard-print suit and top hat, and of course covered in jewellery, was Money Man.

'There are many beautiful masks here today,' he said into a gem-encrusted megaphone, 'but the most beautiful is . . . MINE!'

He pointed at his own mask and smiled, his gold tooth glinting in the sun.

'Looking this good doesn't come cheap, so please donate to my Keep Money Man Beautiful fund.'

The crowd stood silent, stunned by what they were seeing.

Then money started flying from the pockets and purses of the people standing closest to Money Man. Two men were lifted high by their pockets, and landed with a thud when their cash flew out towards Money Man's outstretched hands.

That's when the screaming began.

People started stampeding away from Money Man and his float, shoving each other out of the way as they ran.

Penny turned . . . but Ethan was gone!

She looked around for him, and then saw E-Boy, helmet and all, step from around a corner.

'Are you sure?' she yelled above the noise of

the panicked crowd. 'We've really got to get to that airfield . . .'

Ethan shrugged. 'Someone has to stop him,' he said. 'Get somewhere safe.'

As Penny dashed away, he ducked under the barrier, stepping out in front of the float.

'Please give generously, everyone,' Money Man was shouting, 'because it won't hurt as much as when I take it! Be happy that you're part of history, as this has to be the biggest—'

He stopped, and looked at Ethan. His smile twisted into anger.

'You AGAIN?!' he yelled, the megaphone distorting the scream. 'Can't a man make a simple living without Captain Antenna messing things up?'

'You need to leave these people alone,' said Ethan.

He kept his gaze on Money Man, but could hear hurried feet and doors slamming to his right. He assumed it was happening on his left as well.

'And you,' said Money Man, 'need to stop messing with my income! Well, this time it's for the last time!'

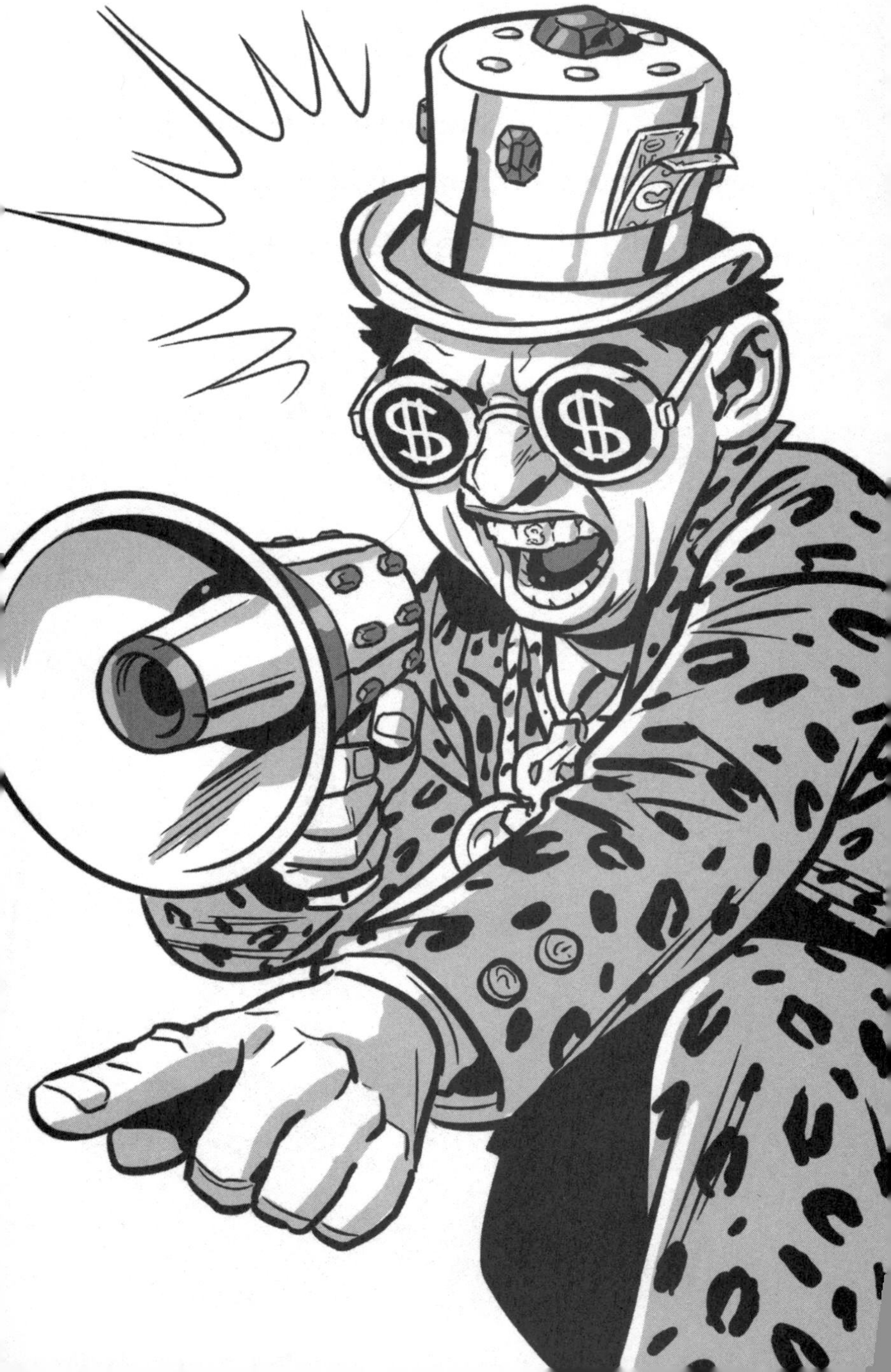

With a click of Money Man's fingers, the coin wheels separated from the float. He pointed at Ethan and the wheels spun through the air at him like frisbees.

Ethan threw himself over a barrier and around a corner. The wheels slammed into the wall and exploded, showering the road with coins.

Money Man grunted in frustration, then looked around. While he'd been busy with E-Boy, the crowd – all his potential victims – had gotten away. His float, which was now actually floating, zoomed down the main street after Ethan.

Penny sprinted to a cafe, along with a group of scared tourists. As soon as the streets looked clear, the owner locked the door.

The owner grabbed a remote control from the bar, and a television mounted high on the wall flicked on. It showed an aerial view of the street outside.

'Again, our coverage of the annual Festi Oculta parade has taken a shocking turn. The criminal known as Money Man has appeared, but there's another mysterious figure here who seems to be— My goodness, Money Man has just launched . . .'

BIG TROUBLE IN DOWNTOWN ALOYA

Penny winced as she watched Ethan's narrow miss, and crossed her fingers as he ran.

Ethan stopped and leant against a wall. He knew Money Man was behind him but couldn't hear anything. He could hear crowd noises ahead – part of the street party must be unaware of what had happened at the parade.

He didn't want to lead Money Man to a new group of people to rob, so he turned right.

Ahead was a construction site. The festival was a public holiday, so the massive machines sat still. Ethan reached out to see if he could move any of them, but he could see no silver streams. *The power must be off.*

Ethan suddenly felt a sharp pain in the back of his head, and heard the *clink* of a coin falling to the ground.

He turned around and saw Money Man, riding his float like a magic carpet.

'Why doesn't your left arm move when you run, Antenna Head?' the villain sneered. 'Maybe you're not as powerful as last time we met?' Money Man gave a wide grin. 'Time for some payback!'

With a flick of his hand, two more coins flew at Ethan. Ethan ran, the sound of Money Man's laugh ringing in his ears.

He found a hole in the fence and scrambled through. A sharp bit of wire snagged his costume, cutting him on the shoulder. He pushed through and sprinted deeper into the construction site.

'Now where could you be running to?' said Money Man, flying over the fence on his float.

Ethan ran past diggers and jackhammers, and found a bulldozer to hide under as Money Man flew past.

Ethan ran from machine to machine, turning them on, careful to keep out of his chaser's sight. He found a small white building with wire over the windows, and the sign *SITE OFFICE* on the door. He grabbed a crowbar that was lying nearby, wedged it into the door next to the lock, and pushed.

'Where are you, Antenna Head?' Money Man's voice taunted him.

Ethan strained, the metal of the crowbar hard against his chest. 'Come *on*,' he grunted.

'You can't hide forever! Everyone pays the Money Man!'

Ethan gave one last push with everything he had, and the door crunched open. He fell into the office and looked around . . . *There*.

The master power switch.

He flicked it to ON, and felt a surge as electricity flowed through the construction site, and its wi-fi and systems came online.

With the network signals flowing and the power on, Ethan felt better than he had in days. His arm still wouldn't move, and his sight and hearing were still poor, but he was a lot less helpless than he had been minutes before.

A plan came to mind.

Penny was biting her nails watching the television.

'Money Man and his mystery opponent appear to have entered a construction site,' said the voiceover. *'Our drone cameras will show us, and you, every step of this strange and fascinating battle.'*

Money Man was losing patience. 'I have tourists to rob, boy! Show yourself and let's get this over with!'

'I'm over here!'

Money Man turned, and stared across an open expanse of freshly laid concrete to where Ethan sat in a digger at the far end.

Money Man fired three coins at Ethan, but they just bounced off the reinforced perspex windows of the digger.

Money Man stood motionless for a moment, then that wide grin came across his face again. All the coins from the wheels and poles of the float, plus the gold coins of the giant glasses, formed into a single massive ball.

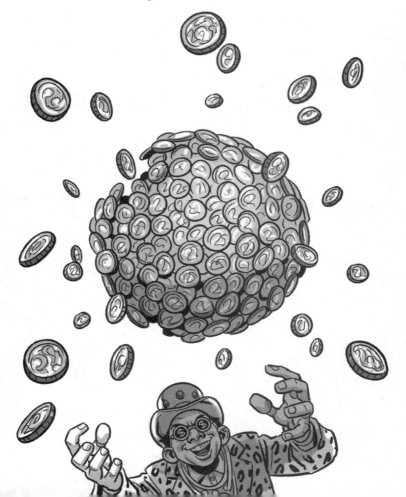

'Say goodbye, Captain Antenna!'

The ball flew at the digger. All that weight of metal, far more than the reinforced perspex could possibly stand, hurtled straight at Ethan.

'It's E-Boy,' said Ethan.

With a thought, he swung a massive wrecking ball from a nearby crane directly at the coin sphere, timing it perfectly.

The heavy balls crashed into each other with a huge, deep *CLANG*.

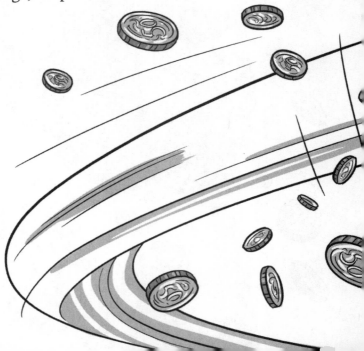

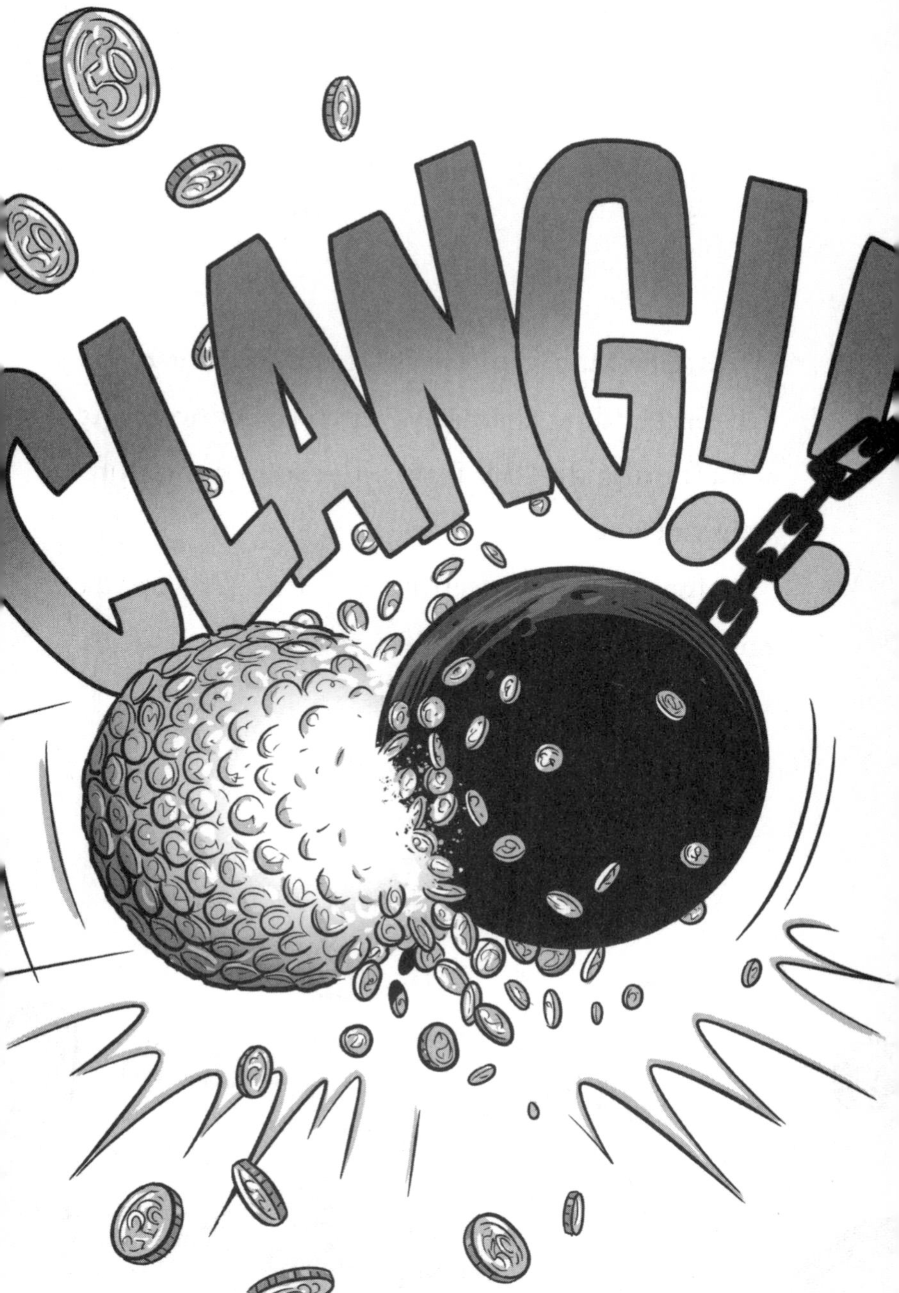
CLANG!!!

Money Man's sphere shattered and the coins fell, embedding themselves into the concrete. It wasn't quite dry, but it was just solid enough to trap the coins in it.

Money Man concentrated hard. Two of the coins returned to him, but the rest were stuck fast.

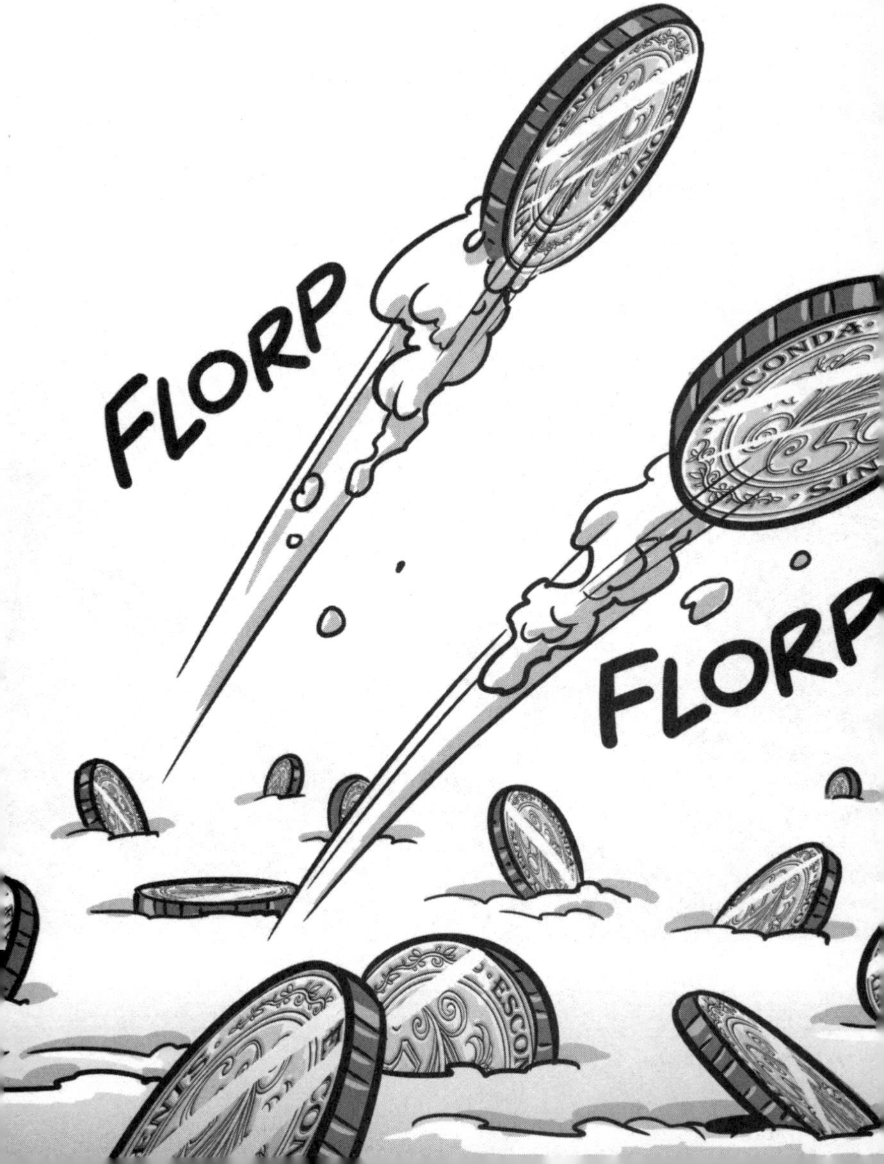
FLORP
FLORP

Ethan sent two bulldozers towards Money Man, rumbling at him from opposite directions, threatening to trap him between their huge scoops. A look of terror crossed Money Man's face.

Money Man flew past them and across the construction site, away from Ethan.

There was a gasp in the cafe as the two metal globes collided, and a cheer as Money Man's money ball shattered. The cheer got louder as Money Man flew away from E-Boy on his disc of flying coins.

Penny grinned as relief ran through her, then looked at the owner. 'Could you let me out, please?'

The cafe owner unlocked the door, and Penny sprinted out.

Ethan stopped focusing on the dozers and smiled . . . then realised that Money Man was flying towards the part of the town where the festival was still in full swing.

A whole new bunch of people to rob!

He jumped down from the digger and ran, following Money Man.

Ethan focused on the automatic gate, and it opened for him to continue the chase.

Back out on the street, Money Man was now walking, trying to be a bit less conspicuous, but still robbing some of the partygoers as he went. One partygoer, a man in a bomber jacket and a devil mask, was dancing on a hotel balcony when Money Man made a grab for his cash. Money Man's power pulled at the partygoer with such force that he fell off the balcony!

Ethan saw that the hotel had a retractable awning over the main entrance. In an instant he'd reached into the hotel's electronics and flung the awning open. The plummeting partygoer's leg tore through the fabric of the awning, but all that hit the ground was his shoe.

Money Man turned and saw Ethan at the fringe of the party. While the dancing raged on, he sent a torrent of cash towards Ethan. A banknote slapped over Ethan's mouth, silencing him, while the rest swirled around him, fluttering like angry birds.

Ethan flailed his right arm around himself while his left flapped uselessly. He heard Money Man's megaphone-amplified voice.

'Aloya! My gift to you, a tornado of money! Simply dive in and take what you want! Grab what you can quickly, though, before your fellow revellers get there first!'

Excited shrieks filled Ethan's one good ear. He could only see vague blurs of people, but knew they were stampeding towards him!

I'm gonna get crushed!

He focused as much as he could in the chaos of flying currency, but he couldn't find any electronics to help him.

'Ethan! ETHAN!'

Was that Penny's voice? Ethan's eyes darted around frantically, and saw a shape that could be her. She looked like she was trying to gesture, but he couldn't tell.

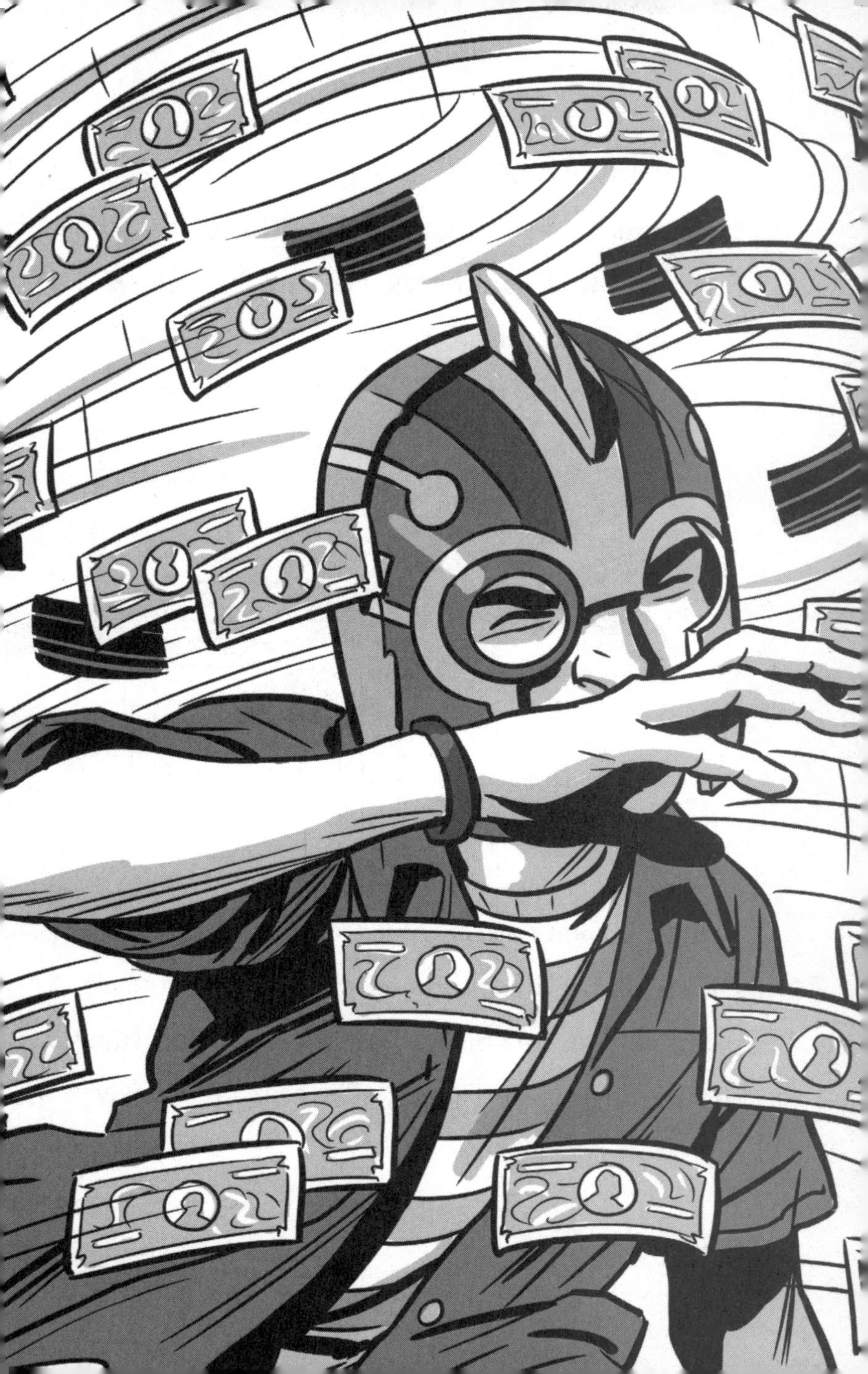

'Ethan! LOOK UP!'

Ethan looked up, seeing nothing but the flurry of more banknotes. He shut his eyes and looked up with his power.

He found the television station's drone.

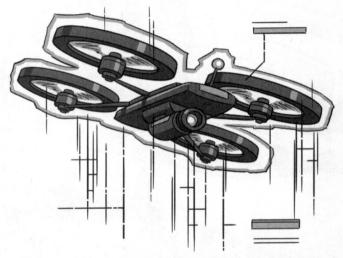

Ethan took control of it and brought it down. He steered it in a tight circle around himself, propellers at full blast. The blast of wind blew the money up and away, scattering it in every direction.

The revellers grabbed at the notes flying every which way, jumping and giggling, and nowhere near trampling Ethan into the ground.

'NOOOOO!' Money Man's shout didn't need his megaphone to be heard over the noise of the festival.

Ethan closed his eyes and looked through the drone's camera, sending it flying after him.

Money Man sent his last remaining coin at the drone, which smashed through the lens and the electronics. Before the drone lost power completely, Ethan sent his power through it, and saw four more drones in the sky over Aloya.

They were not far away. The clash of powers had been the big story of the day. Ethan took control of them and sent them after Money Man.

Money Man ran. He elbowed his way through the crowd and into an alley.

Ethan's nose started to bleed.

Even with his helmet, in his current state he was having trouble controlling four drones at once. He could only make out the barest of glimpses through their cameras. Even so, that was enough for him to be able to watch as Money Man's top hat hit the ground, then his dollar-sign glasses, then his leopard-print jacket.

'Ethan. Ethan. Come back to yourself. He's not worth it.'

Ethan returned his thoughts to his body, and felt Penny gently shaking him. He blinked as she cleaned the blood off his face.

Ethan looked around. People were talking, some were pointing at him, some were smiling, some just looked amazed.

'Ethan, we need to get out of here,' said Penny.

The man in the bomber jacket, now holding his devil mask instead of wearing it, approached them on his Vespa bike.

'I've . . . I've been listening to people talking,' said the man in the bomber jacket. 'The hotel awning . . . it . . . did you . . . did you save me?'

Ethan gave a gesture between a nod and a shrug.

The man grabbed Ethan's hand in a handshake. 'Thank you. THANK you. I . . . I have no words for . . . Let me thank you properly. I'm Diego. What favour can I do for you? Anything, anything in the world!'

'Well, we need to get to Bombara,' Ethan replied.

'Oh my. I didn't mean *that* big a favour!!!'

'Oh no, we just need you to point us in the direction of the airfield,' said Penny.

'Okay, that's eeeeasy!' exclaimed Diego. 'Jump on my chariot and I'll take you there!'

Ethan looked at the little Vespa. It really didn't seem to be big enough to take the three of them.

'C'mon! Just jump on the back!' Diego wriggled forwards on the seat and made a tiny bit more space.

The crowd around them was growing. Penny grabbed Ethan's arm.

'C'mon,' she said. She climbed onto the back of the Vespa and shuffled up against Diego to make space for Ethan to hop on.

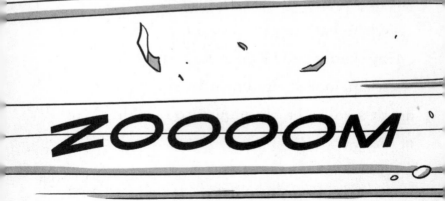

ZOOOOM

'Adios, amigos!' yelled Diego to the crowd as he revved up his chariot, and the gang *put-putted* their way through the streets towards the airfield.

CHAPTER 8

As they approached the airfield, deserted of people on this festive holiday, Ethan carefully surveyed the planes on the tarmac. Most of them were old-style planes with minimal electronic controls. Then Ethan spotted several more modern ones parked near each other.

'Who owns those planes?' he asked Diego.

'They belong to the government,' said Diego.

'Government planes. We could just borrow one?' Ethan said to Penny.

'We don't have much choice,' she replied.

'I suppose they can retrieve it from Bombara once we're done with it.'

'What are you two talking about?' enquired Diego.

'Nothing, Diego. We're just talking rubbish,' said Ethan. 'Could you let us off here, please?'

Ethan and Penny said goodbye to Diego and made their way to the bunch of government planes.

As they got closer to the planes Ethan felt around the electronics of the individual aircraft, and picked out a single-engine Cessna.

Ethan hacked the electronic lock with ease, and the plane's door flipped open.

As they climbed into the plane, Ethan's foot slipped on the step. Penny caught him. 'Are you okay?' she asked.

'I'm okay,' said Ethan, but they both knew he was lying. He was weaker than ever, and the sight in his left eye was completely gone.

'Are you sure you can do this?' asked Penny.

'It's one device. I can do it. You might need to hold the steering wheel for a while.'

Ethan made his way to the pilot's seat and slumped into it. Penny clicked his seatbelt together as he closed his eyes and sent his thoughts through the plane, becoming familiar with its systems. He actually felt a little better as he focused completely on the plane, leaving his own body behind.

Ethan commanded the engine into action, and within minutes the small plane was lifting off.

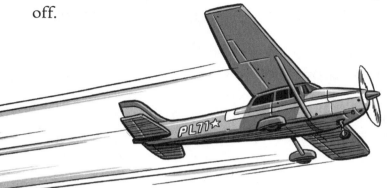

Looking through the plane's forward cameras made Ethan feel like it was just him and the open air. The plane soared higher into the blue, and for a moment Ethan forgot that Penny was even there.

The Cessna glided over the parade below, towards the beautiful green mountains in the distance. Ethan felt like a huge eagle soaring through the sky. He was enjoying the freedom, the fluffy clouds in the distance, the . . .

'ETHAAAAAN!!!' Penny screamed.

Ethan's eyes snapped open to see something terrifying on the other side of the windscreen.

Gemini was staring back at him from the outside of the plane!

TO BE CONTINUED . . .

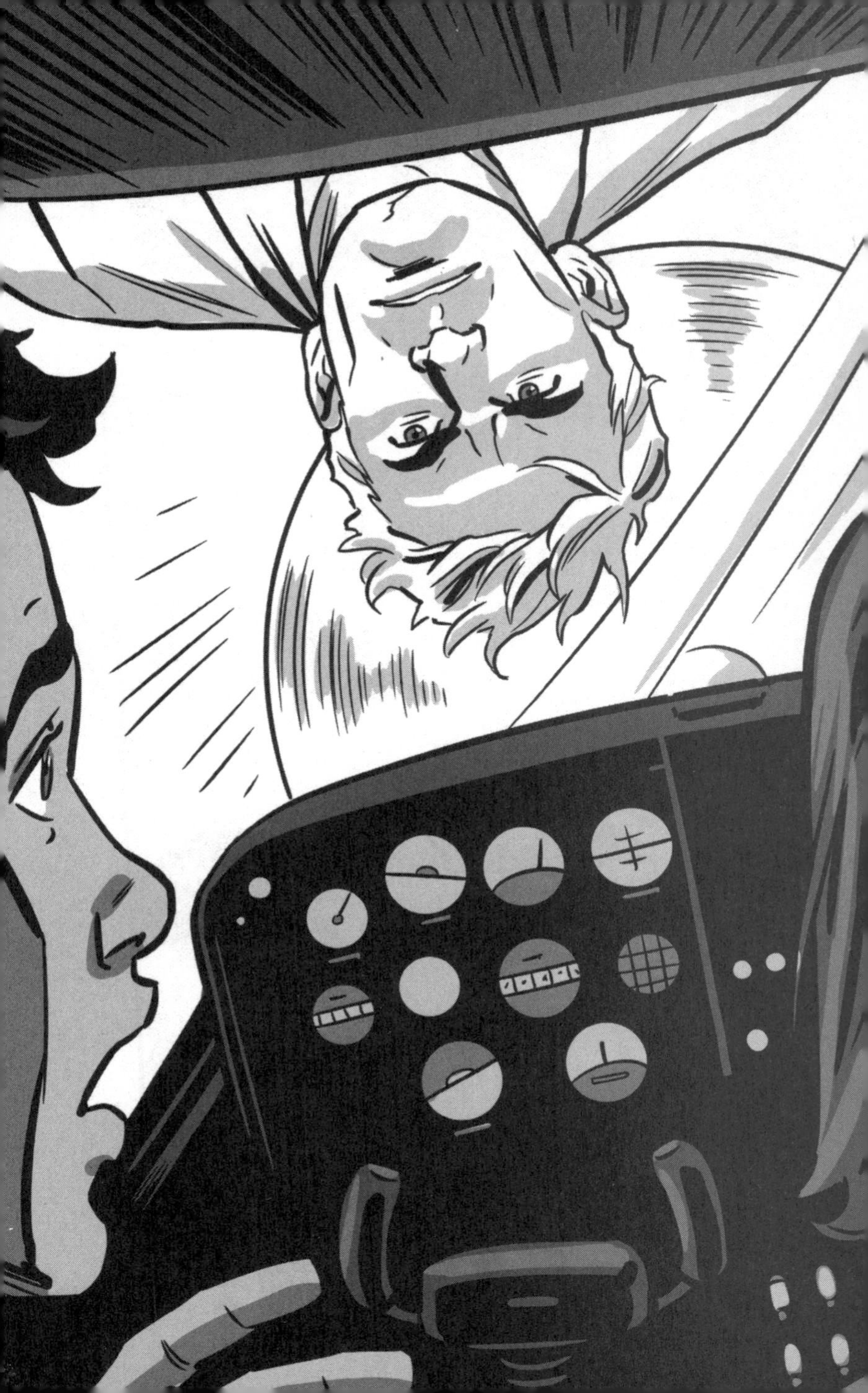

E-BOY 4

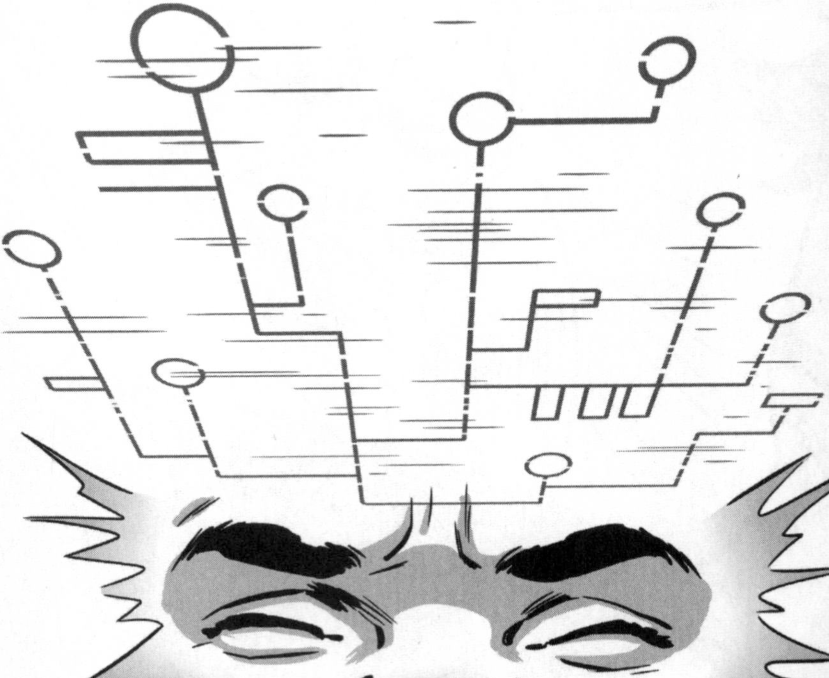

COMING SOON!